crossing *the* hudson

PETER STEPHAN JUNGK

crossing the *hudson*

— a novel —

translated by
David Dollenmayer

HANDSEL BOOKS
an imprint of Other Press · New York

Klett-Cotta © 2005 J.G. Cotta'sche Buchhandlung Nachfolger GmbH, Stuttgart. Originally published in German as *Die Reise über den Hudson*

The translation of this work was supported by a grant from the Goethe-Institut that is funded by the Ministry of Foreign Affairs of the Federal Republic of Germany.

"Mercedes Benz" lyrics on page 9 by Janis Joplin, Michael McClure, and Bob Neuwirth; recorded by Janis Joplin (Columbia Records, 1971). "I'm a Believer" lyrics on pages 22 and 23 by Neil Diamond, recorded by The Monkees (RCA, 1966). "There's a Kind of Hush" lyrics on page 24 by Les Reed and Geoff Stephen, recorded by Herman's Hermits (MGM Records, 1967).

Translation copyright © 2008 David Dollenmayer

Production Editor: Yvonne E. Cárdenas
Book design: Natalya Balnova

This book was set in 11.5 pt Bembo by Alpha Design & Composition of Pittsfield, NH.

10 9 8 7 6 5 4 3 2 1

Library of Congress Cataloging-in-Publication Data

Jungk, Peter Stephan, 1952–
    [Reise über den Hudson. English]
    Crossing the Hudson / Peter Stephan Jungk ; translated by David Dollenmayer.
        p. cm.
    ISBN 978-1-59051-275-3
    I. Title.
    PT2670.U53R4513 2009
    833'.914—dc22

                                                              2008022289

Publisher's Note:
This is a work of fiction. Names, characters, places, and incidents either are the product of the author's imagination or are used fictitiously, and any resemblance to actual persons, living or dead, events, or locales is entirely coincidental.

Like a bridge over troubled water
I will lay me down.

— Paul Simon

crossing the hudson

1

Mother was pressing the woman in the red uniform to hurry up. "We're just about at the end of our rope. My son has been on the go for twenty-nine hours straight. He can't keep up like this—don't you understand? Just take one good look at him and you can tell. We've been waiting in this line for fifteen minutes . . . There's only three of you even though you're besieged by customers . . . I'd like to speak with your supervisor . . . No, I can't calm down and I won't calm down . . . I told you we should take a taxi, Gustav . . . No, he didn't have to spend the whole twenty-nine hours in the plane, not that, thank God, right Gustav?"

Gustav nodded. Or did he shake his head?

". . . but he doesn't have as much stamina as other men his age. He's had a heart operation and he was often sick as a child . . . You found it finally? A Pontiac? Gustav? Why not. What color is it? . . . You don't know? . . . Rubin. With an *R*, that's right. No, not with a *B*. Bubin—come on, what kind of a name would that be? Sounds ridiculous. No wonder you couldn't find the reservation . . . Pardon me?"

The clerk at the rental car agency repeated her question very loudly, as if mother and son were hard of hearing.

"One of the engines broke down over the Atlantic," Gustav answered quietly. "They replaced it overnight."

"You don't have to apologize for being tired! They put him up in the only airport hotel in Reykjavik."

"They put us up in the airport hotel . . ." Gustav echoed.

"What do you mean 'us'? I thought you were flying alone. Who were you with?"

"I meant . . . the other passengers . . . and me . . ."

"He hardly slept at all. It doesn't get dark there all night long and he left his sleep mask at home," Mother explained to the young woman. "The airline gives all the passengers sleep masks, but if he doesn't have his own mask—a marvelously soft one, from Hermès, a present from me for his fortieth birthday—then it's just plain awful for him. He's so used to his own things, he can't sleep with a brand-new mask that still has that factory stink."

The lady from the rental car agency was rolling a ballpoint pen back and forth on the surface of the tall counter with the tip of her index finger, her curved fingernail with purple nail polish scraping along the Formica.

"Please stop that," said Mother. "It gives me the shivers. It goes right to the center of my nerves."

Gustav had been fearful when the female pilot of the wide-bodied jet announced she had to land in Reykjavik because of a technical problem. They were halfway between the coasts of Ireland and Iceland and she preferred not to turn around. He'd been afraid of flying for years and suffered acute trepidation days before each departure. Still, sitting in the middle of row 17, he took the announcement more calmly than most of his neighbors. Some turned pale, shaky. They held on to their companions or hugged their children tight. Solitary travelers looked at each other with frightened faces; others started up conversations. More than once he heard the remark, "No wonder, a woman driver!" Two corpulent men in business class had fainted. He peered through the gap in the curtain and saw them stretched out on the cabin floor, surrounded by a steward and three stewardesses.

"Credit card and driver's license?" said the employee of the rental car agency.

He asked for her ballpoint pen, put his signature in one little box and his initials, GRR, into the others. The young woman handed the key to his mother and described how to get to the eighth level of the parking garage, located two terminals away. Easy to find, she emphasized. For someone who makes the trip from the rental car office to the parking garage several times a day, the eighth level of the parking garage at John F. Kennedy International Airport is undoubtedly easy to find. Gustav and Mother, on the other hand, got lost. Pulling the two heavy, oversized suitcases behind them, they had to

3

retrace their steps, ask again, and when they were finally in the right terminal, they couldn't find the elevator that was supposed to go to the eighth level.

They were standing by their car at last, a blood-red Pontiac Grand Am that looked like the pimp cars in Vienna parked every three or four hundred yards along the street. No, not parked, but left standing at a tilt, with their right front and rear wheels up on the sidewalk.

"Out of the question, Gustav. What a hideous car! I can't stand it. Get a different one," Mother exclaimed.

He didn't have the strength to go back to the rental office and get a more acceptable model. Or, if it had to be a Grand Am, then at least in another color. He wanted to get to Carmel as quickly as possible, where his anxious family had been waiting for him since the day before. Mother had come to the airport twice for nothing. Each time, they told her that her son's plane would be landing very much behind schedule. If she had been told the whole truth at that point, she probably would have had a breakdown. She insisted on picking him up instead of waiting for him in her apartment on Central Park West. "If you're really so tired," she now declared, "I'm not going to let you drive. Absolutely not."

The trip to the lake house would take two, perhaps two and a half hours at most, he figured. On Friday afternoons there was heavy traffic on New York roads, the divided highways fanning out toward the Hamptons, upstate, to Connecticut and Massachusetts. He had often covered the stretch from the airport to their vacation house on Lake Gilead in ninety minutes, but never on a Friday. He'd booked the flight so he would arrive on Thursday. On principle, he never took an international flight on a Friday.

With some difficulty he stowed the luggage away in the much too cramped trunk and got in behind the wheel, feeling like an astronaut in a space capsule. Mother sat rigidly beside him. He felt sorry for her, so squeezed in, her face grimly set, justifiably indignant that he hadn't given in to her wish that he ask for a different car.

He drove down eight levels of the spiral ramp to the ground floor, enjoying the automatic transmission, and had no trouble finding the correct exit from the airport. He turned on the radio "where the news watch never stops. Give us twenty-two minutes and we'll give you the world."

"Do we have to? I've been listening to the news all day," Mother remarked. "You almost crashed. That's enough news for one day."

He turned off the radio, discovered a CD player in the dashboard. He'd been annoyed since takeoff at his own forgetfulness: when he opened up his carry-on bag in the plane, he discovered he'd left his music at home. He was late and in a hurry—the taxi was already honking outside—and Gustav had forgotten his prayer book and his CDs in their transparent plastic sleeves on his bureau in the bedroom.

He was fiddling with his cell phone, confident he could use it without affecting his driving.

Mother jumped on him. "You can't do two things at once. Please stop that, it's terribly dangerous."

"We're already in the car, Madeleine . . . You're right, my one and only love, 'already' is a laugh. A whole day late. A gruesome trip. You better believe it . . . Mother's fine, I think. Right, Mom?" She didn't respond. "No, my angel, I'm not especially tired . . . Don't worry. No police in sight for miles around. Mad, please *Schatz*, it's only a short call . . . Of course I know how much a ticket costs . . . You're right, I should have called from the parking garage. But who knows if I could have gotten a signal there. So, I'll be there by four, four-thirty at the latest. When does Shabbat begin? When? And lighting the candles? 8:03? All right, 8:03. Wait a sec, Mama wants to talk to you." He handed her the phone.

"You and your Shabbat. My son an Orthodox Jew, I still can't believe it . . . Sorry, what? I already told him he shouldn't use the phone while he's driving . . . What? He looks awful. Like someone spit him out. And he rented the most ghastly car you can imagine. A pimp's car . . . No, I won't fight with him. How are the children? . . . Amadée's swimming? And no one's lifeguarding him? What's Julia up to? You're down by the dock? Well, that's good."

When the call was over, she looked sideways at her son, reproachfully. "The cell phone stays with me from now on. You're completely wound up! And what's 'lighting the candles' supposed to mean?"

"You were already at our house once for that, Mother. It's when we light the candles for Shabbat, the moment that separates the previous week from the day of rest. Madeleine lights the candles, then she spreads out her arms above them and draws them in three times in a circular motion to show that she embraces the sanctity of the Shabbat. Then she puts her hands over her eyes and says the blessing. Do you remember now?"

"My son an Orthodox Jew! Unfathomable . . ."

Manhattan appeared, the line of skyscrapers enveloped in a grayish yellow haze. As soon as the city came into view, he always had the expansive feeling of coming home. It flowed down into his belly and his legs. Nothing like this happened to him anywhere else. He was driving through Jamaica. Forty-five years and three months ago, on May 11, 1954, he'd been born not far from here, in the Elmhurst Hospital in Queens. He'd grown up in Europe: his parents, both émigrés, didn't want to have a foreigner for a son, someone who played baseball or basketball in college and couldn't speak their native language, someone who was just an American.

His gaze fell on the hood of the Grand Am again. Madeleine would reproach him too: You say you weren't tired, so why didn't you go back to the car rental place and ask for a different car? Please! You got here a whole day late anyway. The ten minutes it would have cost you to go back wouldn't have made a bit of difference! Now we have to put up with this abomination for a whole month.

"Did you eat anything at all? Aren't you hungry?" Mother wanted to know. "It's not Yom Kippur today!"

"There was plenty of food on the plane."

"Me, I'm a *bissel* hungry, I've got to admit. Maybe we could make a quick stop somewhere."

"Mother, please! I want to get home as soon as possible—"

"Don't be so whiny. Anyway, you're too fat. It looks almost like baby fat. Doesn't it bother your wife that you're getting a little plump lately?"

"Mother, please—leave me alone—I'm not fat, I'm really not."

Instead of being patient and staying on the Van Wyck Expressway, which crosses the Whitestone Bridge and then turns into the Hutchinson River Parkway, the fastest route north, Gustav turned off onto Grand Central Parkway.

"What are you doing, Burschi? Why are you going this way?"

To his annoyance, this mistake was heading them straight for Manhattan.

"This is just going to cost us more time," Mother griped. "You're the one in such a hurry, not me."

There was no hope of turning around in the quickly moving expressway traffic, and the exit where they could reverse direction was miles ahead. (On the expressways of this world, he often couldn't resist the thought that all the other drivers were as lost as he was.)

He stopped at a gas station and looked at the map.

"Don't you have a better one than that? Just the one from the car rental agency? Don't you have a real map along? You always claim to know your way around so well you can find the way home in your sleep. You've had your Shangri-La for eight years now. You've been there fifteen or sixteen times, and you still don't know how to get there? I think you're doing this on purpose, just to make me extra nervous. As if I hadn't already been through enough today. It's just like you: you always have to tool around the block no matter what city you're in, but then you always get lost. And you've been doing it ever since you learned to drive: always around the block, always in circles. What a disaster."

When he thought he'd figured out the right way to go from the map, he got out of the car.

"Where do you think you're going?"

He slammed the door.

In a rack in the gas station, he found a copy of one of the CDs he'd left at home and also bought nuts, raisins, cookies, a can of Coke.

Inside the car a voice was droning, croaking, wailing.

> *Oh Lord, won't you buy me a Mercedes Benz?*
> *My friends all drive Porsches, I must make amends.*
> *Worked hard all my lifetime, no help from my friends.*
> *So oh Lord, won't you buy me a Mercedes Benz?*

"That's really getting on my nerves, Gustav. You can listen to it when you're traveling by yourself, not with an eighty-one-year-old woman in the ejection seat of this torture chamber of an automobile. Just because my dear son doesn't care enough about me to go exchange a car that is absolutely unacceptable."

She tore open two of the bags, scattering raisins and nuts onto the rubber floor mats. She tossed the contents of the little packets from her cupped hand into her mouth.

"Well? What about that screechy woman? Are you going to turn her off?"

He turned the music down, crossed the Triboro Bridge after paying $2.50 at the toll booth, then continued west, across town, toward the Henry Hudson Parkway. That was a road he knew. It was the highway he sometimes took to get from downtown Manhattan to the house on the lake.

"By the way, do you have an undershirt on?"

"It's unbearably hot, Mother."

"You'll catch a chill if you don't wear an undershirt. An undershirt absorbs moisture from your body and equalizes your body temperature."

"You've been telling me that for as long as I can remember. You're right. But I feel better without an undershirt."

"Your papa always had an undershirt on. And he loved that comfy warm feeling."

With her left hand, Mother reached for the radio's volume knob and turned it off. "You've really gained weight since last spring, Burschi. You've got to watch out or the fat will just come bulging out. And then when you wear one of those baseball caps you have so many of, you'll look like a giant baby. Sorry, but I've got to tell you, because probably nobody else will."

"Madeleine thinks I'm handsome the way I am."

"First of all, she has no taste. And second, she doesn't want to hurt your feelings."

"You, on the other hand, do want to hurt my feelings."

"Not at all. I only want you to feel good about yourself. Your ears aren't very pretty. Have I ever told you that? You've got no earlobes—awful. And to tell you the truth, the back of your neck's a little chubby . . ."

"Will you please stop it now?"

"And such thin, colorless, kind of nebbishy hair . . ." She giggled.

"Mother!"

"What's wrong? You want me to lie to you?"

At the corner of 125th Street and Park Avenue, a large sign for one of the in-town offices of the car rental chain caught their attention. "Pull over right here and go see if we can get a different car."

In front of the plate-glass windows of the branch office stood a wide, snow-white car, gleaming in the pale sunlight. It had just been washed and the last drops of water were sliding off onto the asphalt. Gustav pulled over into the right-hand lane and took a look at the car from close up, a late-model Cadillac DeVille which instantly enchanted him. He entered the empty office. "Hello?! Anybody here? Hello!" An older man with white hair and a freshly pressed uniform emerged from the men's room fastening the top button of his fly and apologizing. Gustav pointed to the Grand Am standing in the second lane. Mother waved to them from the car. He explained that he had rented the car an hour ago at the airport but that he was very unhappy with the color. Would it be possible, he asked, assuming his wish was unfulfillable, to exchange the red Pontiac for that white Cadillac? And if he could trade, how much more per month would the Cadillac cost than the Pontiac?

"I don't particularly like my color, either," the old man chuckled, shaking his head. He remarked that personally, he liked the red car much better than the white one. He leafed through a thick volume. "Hundred and thirty-three." Per day? Per week? "Per month, Dear." For one month the lily-white Cadillac cost $133 more than the carnation-red Pontiac. Gustav signed a new contract, handed over his credit card again, and thanked the clerk as gratefully as if he had revealed the magic password granting access to a cave full of treasure. He heaved the two suitcases into the Cadillac's large trunk, helped Mother into the new car, and parked the Grand Am in a space toward which the man in the red uniform, who had stepped out of the door of the office, was vigorously gesturing. They switched cars and took off as if floating on air.

"He looked very nice, the rental car Negro," Mother declared. "That would have been your chance to put on an undershirt."

The heaviness in his limbs, the soft, spongy feeling in his knees, the fog around his temples—by-products of jet lag still characteristic of intercontinental travel at the end of the twentieth, beginning of the twenty-first century—they all fell away from Gustav. Seldom in recent months had he had a moment of such satisfaction as on this Friday afternoon, August 6, 1999, the fifty-fourth anniversary of the dropping of the atomic bomb on Hiroshima.

Thirty-five years ago, he had felt a comparable high at the skating rink in Vienna, between the unfathomably deep excavation for the future Hotel Intercontinental and the auditorium of the Musikverein, across from his school, the Akademisches

Gymnasium on Beethovenplatz. He was gliding across the ice, swift and elegant, adroit and fast, like the figure skaters doing their jumps in a roped-off area. He pretended to be Danzer, the world champion, whom he had watched practicing double loop jumps, putting on a demonstration to the strains of a waltz by Johann Strauss. And then came the most beautiful part: in his exit glide after completing the jump, Danzer pulled off his supple black leather gloves, very slowly, very gradually. After the left glove was removed, he carefully took off the right one. Gustav imitated the way he did it—this loving removal of his gloves during the exit, while gliding off the ice. The same feeling flowed through him now, behind the wheel of the snow-white 1999 Cadillac DeVille.

"God, what a terrible car that other one was," Mother complained.

"But let's not talk about it anymore. And you shouldn't take the name of the Lord into your mouth for such trivialities."

"You call that trivial? And what do you mean, take it into my mouth? The word 'God' isn't a piece of sausage or toast, is it? At least admit that it was a hideous car."

2

They drove north. He turned the radio back on, 1010 WINS New York, where the news watch never stops. A short report from the home of Mariah McWilliams in Yonkers, a former cook and domestic worker who was celebrating her 104th birthday today. "I just kept on living," she informs the crowd of well-wishers. She never married and never had children, "'cause that kills you!" An hour earlier, a thirty-three-year-old Mexican immigrant had shot himself on the pedestrian walkway of the Brooklyn Bridge in full view of the horrified passersby. The ambulance took him to NYU Downtown Hospital, where he was pronounced dead on arrival. "He knelt down so strangely, like an Indian," reported an eyewitness, "then he took a pistol out of his belt and bang, right in the temple."

"Would you please turn that back off? I asked you before: no radio, no music."

There was no CD player in this car, just a tape deck. He realized he'd left the Janis Joplin CD in the Pontiac; he was annoyed.

"Why are you grunting like that, Gustav?"

"Nothing. It's nothing."

"Did you forget something? In the other car?"

"It doesn't matter . . ."

Going back was unthinkable. One more example of the little episodes of absentmindedness that had been crosshatching his life with imprecision since Father's death.

He pressed the button on the radio again, didn't notice that the Henry Hudson Parkway was becoming wider, stayed to the right, in the far right-hand lane, and suddenly found himself by accident on the entrance ramp to the George Washington Bridge. The traffic was flowing smoothly onto the upper level and then in both directions on the eight lanes of the mile-long suspension bridge.

"I don't understand how anyone can pay so little attention. Look where we are now! If you didn't have the radio on, this never would have happened. Couldn't you have paid better attention?"

Suspended above the water, between supporting towers that were as tall as high-rises, he enjoyed the rhythmic shadow play of the steel struts and cables that accompanied his progress on both flanks as well as overhead. He cast sidelong glances at the Hudson River glittering far below, at this point actually half estuary, half river. A few miles to the south, where the Statue of Liberty rises into the sky, the Hudson flows into the Atlantic. In his ears a whoosh and hum, the sound of thousands of tires on the deck of the mighty bridge. They glided off beneath the second tower; he was sorry to have to leave the George Washington Bridge so soon. The trip across it had lasted barely a minute.

"But now we're on the wrong side," Mother complained, "in New Jersey, Slumberland for the less well-off. Please, Burschi, turn around."

He didn't turn around.

They were making good progress, heading north on the Palisades Interstate Parkway. How green it was on the west side of the Hudson, much prettier than on the east side. Little meadows alternated with forestland. A parklike landscape, scenic view pullovers at regular intervals with expansive prospects across the river.

Gustav figured he'd be hugging his family in an hour. His five-month-old daughter, his nine-year-old son, the wife he loved so dearly. Did he love her so dearly?

"But not like in the first few years," Mother remarked—it's true she had fabulous hearing, but he hadn't said a word out loud. "Because that just doesn't happen. It's unheard-of. That only happened with your parents. You can't love her as much after ten years as you did in the beginning. You were happy with her for two years, then you started to get bored, am I right?"

"What are you talking about, Mother?"

"About your wife. You were just thinking about the two of you, weren't you? Papa and me, we really loved each other, and not just like siblings, which is often the case with older couples. No, we really loved each other, right up to the end. Papa liked to smooch and sleep with me. We did everything together, everything, just like at the beginning. I'm sure that's not the way it is between you and your Em." She always referred to Madeleine as Em. "Ludwig had it so good with me, because I entertained him, made him laugh. In all those years with me, he never got bored. And by the way: he was never unfaithful to me because I always made him happy. He didn't need anything but me."

"May I remind you that you told me as recently as five years ago you couldn't take it anymore? That you definitely wanted a divorce? You forgot that part."

"You're making that up. I'd like to know why you try to spread such *myths*. What do you get out of it? How does it help you? Since you're not as happy with your wife as I was with Papa, you want to run down our happiness after the fact?" It was Mother's habit to emphasize several words in each sentence. In that way, trivialities gained central importance. Almost every one of her pronouncements resonated with something dramatic, final, and absolute, however unimportant it might prove at second glance.

He asked Mother to call the vacation house. She pressed the redial button.

"I'm getting the answering machine . . ."

"This is the Rubin summer residence . . ." His son's high, serious voice. He spoke perfect English. "Sorry we're not in right now . . . please leave us a message after the beep . . ."

"It's me, your grandmother," Mother said into the recorder. "We're halfway there already. Gustav got lost again of course, same as always. See you soon, *Kinder!*"

"Don't mix languages!" Father had always warned him, "or you'll end up talking pidgin when you grow up. Speak either English or German, but not this émigré gibberish." Ludwig David Rubin couldn't stand it that so many of the refugees from Eastern Europe who had settled in Germany and Austria after the war was over—survivors of genocide like himself—decades later had still not managed to learn to speak perfect German. He had no qualms about calling out an angry *Lernen Sie Deutsch!* to his fellow survivors as soon as he found himself subjected to their Yiddish-attacks, as he called their cascades of talk in Eastern European accents.

They weren't far from Nyack. Large signs directed them toward a bridge that he knew only by name. TAPPAN ZEE BRIDGE was written in large white letters on a green background. Their first chance since the George Washington Bridge to cross back over the river and continue their trip to Carmel on the east side. He merged the snow-white car into the right lane so he could take the right fork.

The highway wound in serpentines down to the Hudson, wide as a lake here at Nyack. The road reminded Gustav of the gentle descent to Trieste as you approach the city from the hill country. There too the driver, coming down from the mountainous Karst region, feels like he's landing a glider. Half-way down the mountain the first suburbs appear and one looks down at the sea, the harbor, the geometric grid of the streets, draws nearer to the center of the city with each successive curve. Trieste—city at the edge of the Alps, city by the sea, magical city, crossroads of humanity, a city Gustav loved like no other in Europe, the birthplace of the maternal grandparents he'd never known and whose graves he couldn't visit, their ashes gone with the wind over a provincial Polish town.

Tappan Zee. He had had no idea how big the bridge was, twice as long as the George Washington. Soon he would reach the causeway supported by dozens of concrete pilings and leading in a rising curve to the higher, steel-strutted middle section. In a broad reverse curve, the cantilever bridge then swung gently back down to the opposite shore of the Hudson. It lay in the water, the Tappan Zee, like a gigantic snake. In the middle, huge steel trusses towered into the sky, the two sides mirroring each other, rising to a point like a mountain peak above each tower—or like the dorsal fins of a dragon? The S-shaped skeleton of a monster with two tall, bony projections rising from its back. From this distance, it reminded Gustav of the structures he used to build as a boy on the parquet floor of his room, using Matador wooden blocks with holes bored in them so you could fasten them together with little dowels.

"You can have this whole landscape here. I don't care for it," Mother remarked. "I don't see how you can spend your vacation here every year. It's nice for me, of course, because then I get to see you, but why do you find it so beautiful here? Compared to the landscape in Austria. I just wouldn't be me without that Austrian beauty. It's so fantastic in the Salzkammergut, at the lakes, in the woods, the mountains, everywhere. Sometimes I get so homesick for it. The pink mountains in the sunset, the air so sweet and fresh and mild. But for his work it was important for Papa to be here often, because of his teaching jobs. Too bad. What I don't miss are the people—those Austrians. Not them! God, what awful people."

"I live in Austria, Mother. Perhaps I should remind you of that from time to time."

"You live there. To earn money, yes, I know. It's a shame you're there, you poor thing. Probably because Em wants to be."

"Mom, Madeleine would much rather live here in America . . ."

"Hmm," Mother said, "ah well."

He was looking forward to driving across the bridge. He'd glide across the Tappan Zee, sail over it like the hawks circling above the river. They had their nests on top of the towers, placed there by the New York State Thruway Authority to scare off the pigeons who fouled the beams with their droppings unless they were chased away.

He opened the window. Air-conditioning enervated him. It annoyed him that the motor had to consume gas to cool down the air.

"Do you mind—?" he asked Mother.

She was asleep, having nodded off after their last exchange. Now he heard a quiet clicking sound—exactly! That sound she made so often in her sleep! When he was a boy and they were traveling, he would share a hotel room with his parents, lying on a wobbly folding cot at the foot of their bed or on a narrow couch. He would wake up while they were still asleep and listen to Father's snoring and Mother's quiet clicking, a snapping between the tip of her tongue and the roof of her mouth, a rhythmic sound like small twigs being broken.

He seldom had to sleep in his own room in a hotel, but when he did, he suffered so much at being separated from his parents, even for just a few hours, that Father had to think up something to make it a little easier for his child to bear being alone at night. He invented the string telephone: he ran a piece of package twine from the parental bed, through the crack under the door of their double room, ran it kitty-corner across the hall and pulled it through the crack under the door of Gustav's single room, five doors down on the other side of the corridor, and tied it tight to a leg of his night table. He said good night to the ten-year-old and went back to his room. Then he tugged on his end of the string and Gustav's night table would hitch an inch or so across the floor. And his son would answer, pull his end of the string, and that would cause little movements in his parents' room, and so on, until Gustav's fear of the dark and of being alone would gradually subside, inch by inch, tug by tug.

As they drew nearer, he saw that the lanes for oncoming traffic were closed for construction. A couple of egg yolk yellow bulldozers were jolting forward and backward. The dull thuds of drilling machines were audible from a considerable distance. The eastbound traffic flowed slowly but steadily. It was shortly before three in the afternoon.

The telephone in Mother's lap jangled and he quickly grabbed it. It was Madeleine.

"We didn't hear you before. Where are you now, exactly? We can hardly wait. Is it still a long way? Amadée wants to know if you're bringing him a present. He's such a marvelous swimmer now, you won't believe your eyes. Did you really get lost, or was she exaggerating again?"

"We'll see you in less than an hour."

"That long still?"

"There's already weekend traffic here, my angel."

"I'm not your angel. I'm your wife."

He pushed the search button. 101.1 FM was playing "I'm a Believer." Gustav turned the music down so as not to disturb Mother's sleep. One of the most important rules of his childhood: don't disturb your parents while they're sleeping! "I'm a Believer"! How he had loved that song when he was twelve, thirteen! Every single verse of it! For weeks, the Monkees' hit was number one on the American and English hit parades.

> *Then I saw her face* (bam bam bam bam!),
> *now I'm a believer.*
> *. . . I couldn't leave her if I tried.*

Every Friday afternoon at six he would sit cross-legged on the floor of his room among his Matadors and Legos, his silver-gray Saba radio tuned to the 49-meter shortwave band. And he would listen to the Top Twenty on the BBC World Service from Bush House. Forever after, that name echoed in his head: Bush House! He compared the ranking of the songs to what it had been the previous week, wrote down the Hit Parade results in special lists he'd drawn up for himself, entered the highest rank of each song, compared it to his own ranking of each hit, or with the rank it reached in England, in Luxembourg, and in the United States.

Back then, he spent every weekly allowance on the most important publication of the British recording industry, the *New Musical Express*, so he could look up every imaginable international listing and enter the most important results in his own lists. "Then I saw her face, (*bam bam bam bam!*), now I'm a believer. . . . I couldn't leave her if I tried." It was about that time that he started touching himself with four fingertips: the thumb and index finger of his left hand and the thumb and index finger of his right. The four fingertips constituted a firm collar which he rubbed up and down near the tip of his penis. The tender pain would grow sweeter and sweeter until suddenly, very suddenly, the high point would come. A delicate drop emerged from the tiny opening of his cock, and he would rub it between the thumb, index, and middle finger of his right hand. Then he lifted the tip of his thumb away from the two other fingertips, ten, twenty times in quick succession and observed the white thread that was formed, thin as a hair. This single spiderweb thread of semen molecules was the connection between his entire being and the future.

One more song from the days of the four fingertips. CBS-FM specialized in oldies:

> *There's a kind of hush all over the world tonight*
> *All over the world you can hear the sounds of lovers in love*
> *You know what I mean*

Herman's Hermits had provided the rudimentary accompaniment to his first orgies of masturbation, as did the Tremeloes and the Troggs, the Kinks and the Animals, the Small Faces and the Doors. It took him months to discover the use of his right hand closed into a fist. But by then he was only touching himself behind his own back, so to speak, for Michael Hess, the best student and best athlete in his class at the Akademisches Gymnasium on Beethovenplatz in Vienna, from a Protestant, Romanian-German family, had been shocked by Gustav's shy revelations. Gustav Robert Rubin! I'm warning you! That causes softening of the brain. You'll lose your mind. By the time you're twenty you'll be confined to a wheelchair, believe me. In a few years you won't be able to sit up straight anymore, won't be able to learn anything, to say nothing of attending university. Stop now, before it's too late! And from then on, Gustav hid behind the side of the armoire where his toys were kept: his Matador blocks, his Legos, his collection of Dinky cars, board games. He stood there, bent over, hidden from the world, rushing toward the shudders of lust.

At the age of twenty-four and two weeks after opening his own law office, Michael Hess, the giant, the best student in his law school class, personally congratulated by the Austrian federal president for his summa cum laude graduation, threw himself off the balcony of his parents' apartment into the inner courtyard of their turn-of-the-century apartment house in Vienna, seven stories below. He was killed instantly. The motive for his suicide: his first and only girlfriend Mariella had accused him of having no idea how to touch a woman and how to make her happy.

The era of the four fingertips. Once, Father returned from a trip twenty-four hours earlier than expected. Gustav had just spread his math homework out on the round teakwood dining room table and turned on the radio. He was hoping to hear one of his favorite hits while he did his work. There was a ring at the door.

He looked through the peephole and was astonished to see the distorted image of his father.

Ludwig bent down and stroked his son's hair, kissed the top of his head. Then he picked up his two suitcases.

". . . lost my keys," he whispered, "last night, in a movie theater in Stockholm."

"How come you're back already? Weren't you going to come home tomorrow?!"

"I flew!" Gustav could smell the alcohol on Father's breath. "They serve you champagne on the plane, you know. And you don't have to pay for it! Is Mommy home?"

Ludwig Rubin's return home a day earlier than expected was as unthinkable as the Danube flowing in the opposite direction or the simultaneous collapse of the two high hills just outside Vienna, the Kahlenberg and the Leopoldsberg. Father never did anything Mother hadn't given him permission to do—anyway, that's what they thought. Mother was afraid of flying. She'd never been in an airplane in her life and forbade her husband and her son ever to board one either. When Father traveled to Japan for his research or—before they moved back to America—when he had to attend a conference or go on a lecture tour, he always took a boat: the *Liberté* or the *Constitution*, the *France* or the *Queen Mary*. He knew them all, the fabled ocean liners.

On the Friday afternoon Father returned a day early, Mother was downtown running errands. She came home two hours later. Father hid in a wardrobe. Mother asked how Gustav's school day had gone. He played the everyday son. "You seem especially tired today, child," she declared, and went into the rooms at the back of the apartment to change, since she never kept on her street clothes at home.

A scream shrilled through the apartment. It sounded like Mother had fallen on a samurai sword. Gustav heard Father's short, dry, goatish laugh. But once Mother had realized it was Ludwig, come back home early, she began to weep and wail the way Arab women do in ritual mourning for a departed loved one. She ran barefoot through the apartment, still in her street clothes above the waist, stark naked below, like a steer escaping its slaughterers at the last moment. Father tried to calm Mother down. He ran after her from room to room. The more he tried to appease her, the greater her anger grew. "Mommy," he pleaded, "please don't act like this. It's not as bad as all that!" He'd called Mother Mommy since Gustav was born. He called her Burschi as well. But then Mother called him Burschi too, and both of them not infrequently called their son Burschi, which could occasionally lead to misunderstandings.

It took Mother several weeks to recover from the shock of her husband's premature return. Since that exceptional day, however, Father traveled almost exclusively by air whenever he had to cover great distances. He never again traveled by ship and much less frequently by sleeping car. Mother, on the other hand, boarded a plane for the first time in her life at the age of fifty-five. And that very first flight from Munich to walled-in West Berlin aboard a four-engine prop-driven airplane of the British European Airlines, as the English carrier was called at the time, was a flight from hell. Never before and only once afterward, as father often remarked later, had he sat in an airplane that shook as violently as that one: it wobbled incessantly and was tossed through the air like a ball by the gusts.

3

The hammering of the drills had swelled to an intense boom-
ing. The bulldozers crept forward and backward, tipping piles
of dirt into dump trucks. It was incomprehensible that they
had closed the three oncoming lanes of the Tappan Zee Bridge
at rush hour. The flow of traffic on Gustav's side of the thruway moved sluggishly toward the approach to the bridge—
not unusual for a Friday afternoon. That's why he never liked
traveling on a Friday. He worried about being home in time
for the beginning of Shabbat, or getting there so late he
wouldn't be able to take a shower and shave before Madeleine
lit the candles.

"How's your ultra-religious friend, by the way?" Mother inquired. She'd awakened from her brief nap. "My God, this racket gets on my nerves! Would you please close the window?"

"I have many religious friends."

"You know exactly who I mean. The one I have to thank for alienating you from me. The one who absolutely had to hook you up with a Sephardic woman and made you marry her instead of you finding a wife for yourself—an Ashkenazi if she had to be Jewish—someone you could really love and truly adore, not just a pious girl who takes everything amiss like she expected something better from life."

"Please don't start in again with that stuff, Mom. I'm happy with her. We're happy with our children."

"That's all you want?"

"Don't always run everything down."

"Me always run everything down? I love you so terribly, terribly much and that's why I say what I feel sometimes. Would you rather have me pretend? That would really be phony!"

With the fingertips of his right hand, he touched the back of his mother's left hand, sprinkled with age spots. She pulled it away. "Brrr! Your fingers are freezing cold! So what's with your friend?"

"He's furious with me because I'll be gone four weeks this time."

"Give me the telephone. I'll call him up."

"He won't answer, Mom. He won't come to the telephone. It's nine at night in Vienna, the beginning of Shabbes."

"Don't say 'Shabbes,' Gustav. It sounds so foreign to me, like you weren't my own child anymore. Tell him to leave you alone. You've got to have a minute or two of vacation! Everybody needs some peace and quiet now and then."

Despite the widespread assumption that the trade in pelts and fur coats comes to a stop in midsummer, furriers actually work tirelessly during the hot months to be well prepared for the profitable business of the fall, Christmas, and winter season. The firm of Lichtmann & Rubin on the Kohlmarkt in Vienna, not far from St. Stephen's cathedral, used the hot time of year for processing the furs they purchased in the spring auctions in Scandinavia, Canada, China, and Russia and selling them to fur dealers all over Austria and—since the revolutions in Eastern Europe—in Poland, Hungary, Slovakia, and the Czech Republic as well.

Now that his three daughters were grown up, Richard Lichtmann never allowed himself to take extended vacations anymore. He was unwilling to leave the business for more than a few days. He begrudged his partner Gustav Rubin a vacation that lasted longer than a week, to say nothing of two. The fur business, moreover, had been in a growing crisis the last few years. The aggressive campaigns of the animal-rights organization PETA had had an effect. More and more often, the shop windows of Viennese furriers were sprayed overnight with red paint, frequently even with blood. Afterward the sidewalks would be littered with fliers denouncing the treatment of foxes, martins, minks, beavers, chinchillas, and rabbits, confined in tiny, filthy cages and awaiting agonizing deaths all over the world—in America, Europe, or Asia.

They'd been in the same class in the Akademisches Gymnasium across from the skating club, Lichtmann and Rubin, but had lost touch after graduation. Richard had moved to Jerusalem to study in a yeshiva, while Gustav went to New York to earn a degree in history and for years thereafter seldom returned to Europe. Soon after his thesis was published, he started to become known in his field. He published articles in American and European scholarly journals in his area of specialization, which had also been the subject of his thesis: "Peace Treaties during the Hundred Years War, 1337–1453." He was gradually making a name for himself.

Back then, he couldn't decide where he wanted to settle down. Would Vienna, Berlin, Paris, or Zurich be his home, or should he live on the East or West Coast of the United States? Up to then, he had basically always lived near his parents, whether in Europe or the States. He had never wanted to be very far from Father and Mother. At the time, the end of the Seventies, Ludwig Rubin, an internationally renowned nuclear researcher and professor of physics, was teaching in downtown Los Angeles at the University of Southern California. Gustav was living in a small bungalow in the Hollywood Hills, surrounded by his books and barely a ten-minute walk from his parents. His father paid the rent. As a result of his scientific work—first and foremost his studies of solar thermonuclear fusion and its potential use as a future source of energy—and thanks to his years of teaching, Father had considerable income at his disposal. Moreover, he belonged to a California think tank with a contract from the federal government to predict future technical and scientific developments as well as their social consequences. The income from this subsidiary occupation alone exceeded by several orders of magnitude what Gustav's profession earned him—or ever would.

One Sunday morning a week after Gustav's twenty-third birthday, father and son were walking along a seldom-used side road in Laurel Canyon when Ludwig asked, "What are you going to live on in the years to come, Gustav? I'm happy to support you just as I have been, if that's what you really want. I'm just not sure that will make you happy in the long run."

At the time, Gustav had about as much money as the average eight-year-old. The woman he was trying to live with reproached him for his apparent lack of any need to be independent and any attempt to establish himself financially. She laughed at him for his pilgrimage to the Great Western Bank at the corner of Sunset Boulevard and Laurel Canyon Boulevard three or four times a month to plunder an account that contained nothing but what Father and Mother had transferred into it. The essays he wrote for prestigious history journals earned him just about enough to take his girlfriend out to dinner from time to time.

"I won't be a burden to you anymore."

Gustav's answer took his Father by surprise. "You're . . . you're not a burden to us."

"Then I must have misunderstood you."

"You certainly misunderstood me. Take your time. I have complete trust in you and your chosen path."

A short time later, he received a letter from his old schoolmate Richard Lichtmann. After his years at the yeshiva, he had returned to Vienna—where he felt at home—and become a junior partner in his father's firm. The proposal he sent in writing seemed at first glance so absurd that Gustav had to read the lines several times before he grasped what was being suggested. One more proof, he thought, how little Lichtmann appreciates—much less respects—the research I've devoted almost ten years of my life to. In the letter from Vienna, dated May 1, 1981, his friend asked if there were any possibility Gustav would be inclined to become his partner in the fur business on the Kohlmarkt. Richard wrote that his father was clearly withdrawing more and more from the daily hurly-burly and he himself could find no one else in Vienna he completely trusted. It was unthinkable to continue the business all by himself. He needed energetic help and it occurred to him to ask his best friend from school to become his partner. "Think," he continued, "of your grandfather Maximilian Fuchs—may God rest his soul—and how he would be dancing for joy in the hereafter to learn of your decision." His last sentences were: "It goes without saying that then you would have no more financial difficulties worth mentioning. My company is the market leader in Austria" (which back then in the early Eighties was in fact still the case), "known and respected throughout the world. So if you agreed to join me in taking on this lovely challenge, you would at last have an assured income, which is—forgive me, but your mother informed me about this on the telephone not too long ago—not particularly the case at the moment." And there was a P.S. which said that Gustav didn't have to decide right away. He could spend one or two months in the shop next summer and make a final decision the following fall.

Gustav thanked his friend for thinking of him, but the proposal was so utterly remote from what constituted his life that he must emphatically and categorically refuse. His passion was history, scrutiny, the search for traces of a time when political Europe had only just begun to take on the contours that still influence our lives today. "No, Richard, don't be angry with me," he closed his letter of reply. "You mean well with your offer, but it's a clear indication of how little you understand me and how much we have drifted apart and lost sight of each other in all these years. It's a shame."

He had barely mailed off the letter when the offer from Vienna, though still strange, suddenly seemed to him not quite so unattractive as it had at first blush. Surely (he now thought), after a certain period of training, wouldn't the profession of a furrier, which of course he would have to learn from the ground up, be compatible with his research? After all, how much time, strength, and attention would it require to sell a few foxes, minks, sables, and beavers? So why not be a furrier by day and continue to pursue his research in the evening, at night, or on the weekends and in his months of vacation?

He talked it over with his parents. Mother encouraged him not to reject out of hand the possibility of a profession that seemed so absurd to him. "Strangely enough, if you did it, you would make me, at least, happy. Because you'd be going into the business I grew up with, in the midst of the stink of pelts, hides, and tanning vats. The fur coats of your Trieste grandfather were the most famous in all Vienna; the soft contours of coats from the house of Fuchs were renowned far beyond Vienna, far beyond the borders of the Habsburg monarchy. I would never have dreamed that a child of mine would continue in my father's profession, but fact is stranger than fiction, no question about it. And I'm sure that in the crates that have been in storage for decades at Kühne & Nagel Shippers in Vienna—crates I never, never wanted to see again for fear of the longing I'd feel for my father if ever I should see his handwriting again—I'm sure that in those crates all his notebooks can be found, everything he wrote down about the profession he loved, books and books written in the tiny, precise handwriting I found so enormously moving and illegible."

There also may have been another motive for Mother's benevolent attitude: her dream of being presented with fur coats once again, as she had been in her girlhood and as a young woman. And besides, by hook or by crook, she wanted to keep Gustav from getting more deeply involved with his girlfriend of the moment, Laurie Zimmer, for she considered Elle (as she called her) a lightweight, "and much too common for you. Just look at her parents, really primitive people, *Geschäftsjuden*—Jewish merchants out for money. They import sweaters, pants, and wool jackets. You can't even see people like that socially, and God forbid you should marry one."

"But that's just what you want to make our Gustav into! You want to turn him into a Jewish merchant like your father!" Ludwig was horrified at Mother's agreement in principle that his only son should learn the trade of furrier.

"Then he'll have something in his pocket," Rosa Rubin, née Fuchs, persisted, "something he can live on if all else fails someday."

35

Father disagreed. "You can't be serious. What could possibly fail? My son, a furrier? Have you both gone crazy? This reminds me of my friend Erwin Chargaff's only son Ted, who became a policeman in Los Angeles. Sure, he specialized in unusual criminal cases, but a policeman! The son of the most important biologist and philosopher of our time, a beat cop! Just like Arnold Schoenberg's son. Poor Arnold Schoenberg! No one knows about this, but Jean Améry's illegitimate daughter became a pedicurist. No wonder he committed suicide. Walter Benjamin, whom I knew well, had only one child, a son. He emigrated to Hong Kong and once there, what did he do but marry a Chinese woman from the city. In the meantime, the son dies and his Hong Kong widow collects enormous sums in royalties every month because she's Benjamin's only heir! Adorno confided to me in tears that his son has opened a pet food store. Of course, Adorno acts as if he has no children, keeps it a secret that he's a father, because he's so ashamed! Ernst Bloch's son Jan Robert is an atrocious good-for-nothing. To this day he doesn't know what to do with himself. He has no profession, probably never will. It's not quite so bad with my friend Herbert Marcuse's children. At least Peter, the oldest, is a professor of urban planning at Columbia. No, but . . . I can't allow it. I won't have people saying that Ludwig Rubin's son is a pelt monger! Everyone will laugh at me, just like I laugh at Messrs. Bloch, Adorno, et cetera. Gustav must continue his research. It doesn't bother me that for the time being he's still living on my—or rather our—money. It can just stay that way until he finds a position as a professor in a few years. As soon as he's published a series of important articles, he'll get a tenure-track job. Please, Burschi, leave him alone. He'll find his way all right. He's our only child in the world, I'm earning good money, why this insanity? What business does a child of ours have slaughtering animals for their pelts? Nobody on my side of the family ever had such a gruesome profession. Just because my father-in-law, a money-hungry Jew of the worst sort, was a furrier, does that mean my son has to be one too?"

But in those days, Gustav was more inclined to follow Mother's advice. He sent a telegram to Richard, asking him to throw the letter that would arrive in a few days into the wastebasket without reading it, and agreeing to a trial month in the summer. He said good-bye to Laurie Zimmer, a librarian at the University of Southern California who took acting lessons in her spare time and wanted to be a movie star. He promised to return to her in five weeks at the latest.

And never came back.

Gustav became a fur dealer, and a successful one at that; the ladies loved him for his charm. With his intuitive empathy, his clever remarks, his ability to give a customer the feeling she was someone special and made an incomparably grand impression in the coat she had chosen, Gustav sold coats of all kinds and all prices to a whole range of women, from the most ordinary to the most distinguished. "We'll have to modify the shoulders a bit and nip it in a touch here at the waist, and the collar should be somewhat wider." And within a few years he had risen to full partner in the firm of Lichtmann, which from then on was called Lichtmann & Rubin. He enjoyed the feeling as the palms of his hands slid over the fur. He liked the unmistakable smell of the storerooms, the concentrated, heavy warmth of the coats under neon lights. His favorite pelts were sable, mink, and Persian lamb. Fine sable, lovely and light as a dream, mink with its extraordinary variations of kind and color, and broadtail lamb, ideal for tailored designs with clean lines.

However, Gustav had no time left to pursue his research— he didn't even have the leisure to read publications or attend conferences dealing with his former area of expertise. When he woke up every morning in the first years of his new life, he had to pinch himself in the arm to make sure he wasn't dreaming, that he really had chosen this professional path and wasn't just imagining it.

4

They drove along the wide, rising curve of the Tappan Zee Bridge. Here the bridge was not yet suspended high above the water, and its support columns stood close together, like the piles of boat landings in Venice or the bridges connecting the Florida Keys. The lanes led gradually upward toward the middle section.

Through the windshield, a mass of Nissans and Hondas, Jeeps and Mercurys, Mazdas, Toyotas, and Volvos from New Jersey and New York, Massachusetts and Florida, Pennsylvania, Connecticut, and Maryland. Behind and beside them, aluminum shapes bulged in all colors and sizes, among them trucks of enormous length and height, their chrome flashing in the sun. A dented, gray tour bus, almost close enough to touch, bore on its rear bumper the broad inscription TAKE YOUR TIME! Motorcyclists were trying to weave their way through the cars, pickups, and minibuses, but the metal hulks stood so close together they couldn't get past: a brand-new tractor-trailer carrying produce with FRESH DIRECT in bright green letters; two identical vans from the Mehadrin Fine Kosher Food company; moving vans, tank trucks, and a battered mobile takeout stand, Joe's Dog House; a Lincoln stretch limo, as snowy white as Gustav's Cadillac but three times as long, its numerous one-way windows mirroring the clouds. The traffic on the bridge rolled forward in slow motion.

"At least you realize what a stupid thing you did? Do you really need someone else to tell you every step to take? If we'd taken a taxi as I suggested, we'd be there already. We certainly wouldn't have gotten onto the wrong side of the river."

"Mother, if you don't get off my back, you're getting out. I'll leave you standing right here in the middle of the bridge, I swear I will. You've been needling me ever since we got in the car."

When they argued in front of other people, which happened quite often, Mother usually first winked at the bystanders and then said, "He just does this to show off as much as he can!" Or she groaned, "My God, when I think how sweet he was as a baby!"

"I need the rental car," Gustav continued. "I can't be without a car all summer. You know Madeleine doesn't have her license, otherwise she could have rented a car when they arrived a week ago."

"Don't get so huffy. What makes you think you're so special? Go ahead and let me out, I'll make out just fine. I'll just walk back to the nearest town and take a train. So what? There's absolutely nothing I hate more than sitting in a traffic jam. I'm starting to feel sick already—these awful exhaust fumes I'm breathing—next thing you know, I'll have to throw up."

Ludwig Rubin had taught his son, "You have to yell at women when they annoy you. When your mother infuriates me, I bellow like a bull and she turns tame as a lamb."

Gustav said nothing.

After a while, Gustav tried to make his voice conciliatory and asked, "Do you want to drive for a while?"

She shook her head. "You call this driving? I call it being stuck. Frozen fast in a sea of metal, frozen . . . in midsummer temperatures. I wish I knew what the trouble was. I hope there's some really dramatic reason for this jam, then at least we can read about it in the paper tomorrow." She took the ever-present bottle of Chanel No. 5 out of her purse, sprinkled a few drops onto her wrinkled neck and dabbed some at her temples. The pungent fragrance pervaded the car. She hunted for her lipstick, couldn't find it, then had it in her hand, screwed it out of its tube, lowered the visor on the passenger side, looked into the narrow mirror, and applied even more red to lips that were already red. Gustav was glad that she wasn't attending to her facial hair with tweezers, as she so often did; since turning sixty, she had little bristly hairs growing around her mouth. Every three or four weeks she had them removed with hot wax, but in between she picked away at them almost every chance she got.

41

"Not a very smart suggestion, my dear. After all, I haven't driven in ten years, not since Papa forbade me to after my little accident," Mother murmured. "Now all of a sudden I should get behind the wheel? I only broke my collarbone, but Father didn't want me ever to drive again. I just can't understand a modern woman like your Em not having a driver's license. That's just unheard of nowadays. It's a mystery to me why you don't see to it that she learns how to drive. How does she go shopping when you're not there? There are no stores anywhere near the lake."

"The neighbors take her along when they drive to the supermarket."

"Idiotic, completely idiotic. I don't want to interfere with your business, but if you had insisted, she would have taken her driving test long ago. But you're a coward; you want to avoid conflict with her. Not like your father at all. If something didn't suit him, he started yelling. And that impressed me."

"On the contrary: the truth is, you resisted even more when he yelled."

"What are you talking about? Not at all! I always subordinated myself to him, always. He set the tone, not me."

There was no vaccination to protect you from Mother's know-it-all attitude. No travel route, no daily schedule, no personal or social conflict was safe from her determination to have a say in the matter. Her apparent omniscience often culminated in the four words "If only you had . . ."

"If only you had insisted that she take driving lessons, she could have picked you up today. Then we would have been spared this whole horrible nightmare . . ."

Father hadn't learned how to drive until he was in his forties, in Brooklyn. And after the fourth lesson the driving instructor was already warning him that his reaction time was too slow for him ever to pass the test. He dismissed Ludwig with a sentence that had become a family byword, "You're a public danger, sir." In the course of the following years, Ludwig had come to regard the automobile with more and more passionate loathing. He began to write letters to the editor. By the end of the Fifties, he was already demanding pedestrian zones in the center of all large cities. Whenever he appeared on radio or television—even when the topic under discussion was unconnected to the skyrocketing increase in the number of vehicles—he took every opportunity to warn of the uncontrolled growth of automotive culture and the crises it would cause. He was passionately worried about increasing air pollution and the ongoing, unregulated disfigurement of the landscape at a time when hardly any public thought was being given to these dangers. Although his life's work was devoted to the search for future energy sources and the risks of an atomic arms race among the great powers, at the beginning of the Sixties Father began to work on a book against "the plague of the late twentieth century." He did research in America, Asia, and Europe for a pamphlet that would brand the automobile the scourge of modern civilization. How beautiful, how peaceful the world would be, he wrote, if our blue planet could one day be free of automobiles again: a fairy-tale paradise. Like so many of his projects, this one never evolved beyond its early stages. He had written the first few chapters. But in contrast to his other half-finished manuscripts, all of which he either lost track of or threw away, Father had kept these pages in the hope of someday completing the book he had begun.

After the family moved to Vienna, they lived in the nineteenth district, in Döbling, on Unterer Schreiberweg at the edge of the Grinzing vineyards, and Father's hatred of automobiles manifested itself in an incident Gustav found out about only after Ludwig's death. His parents had kept it secret for more than thirty years. One night, returning from a vineyard tavern and only a few yards from his garden gate, Ludwig had slipped and hit his forehead against the window of a VW bus parked at the curb. Whereupon he was seized with such a fury against all parked cars that he ran into the house, grabbed an ax from the basement, and flailed away at three of the cars parked on Unterer Schreiberweg. This woke up everyone in the neighborhood; it was after two a.m. Only Mother knew who the perpetrator was, for Father had done the deed very quickly. Despite weeks of investigations by the police, and even though he was the prime suspect and was interrogated several times, nothing could be proved against him. Even less so when, about a month later, Michael Guttenbrunner, a well-known poet in Austria at the time and also armed with an ax, attacked cars parked on Höhenstrasse in Vienna and caused considerable damage. Unlike Ludwig Rubin, Guttenbrunner was caught red-handed. And although he stubbornly denied damaging the three cars on Unterer Schreiberweg, the poet was blamed for this unsolved crime as well.

How down-at-heel and dirty my father's shoes always looked, thought Gustav as he sat there, caught in traffic. There wasn't a single pair in good condition. In his mind's eye, he saw the big toe of his father's left foot through the shriveled, dried-out leather of innumerable pairs of shoes, as if with X-ray vision. In the son's memory, the toenail was always black, yellow, and brown, cracked and unnaturally arched: the result of that night when Father had carried out his auto attack. As he ran back into the house and down the basement steps after the deed was done, the ax had dropped from his hand and onto his left foot. He tripped over the handle and fell full length on the basement floor. Hours later, his big toe was still bleeding. Mother had bandaged it temporarily, because he refused to see a doctor or go to the hospital in the middle of the night. The wound didn't stop bleeding until the following morning. And his big toe never recovered.

In response to Gustav's questions about what had happened to Father's toenail, he was constantly told, "It's always been that way!" although he seemed to recall that before, Father's big toe had looked well cared for and completely normal. Why did they keep the truth from him? Because they told him the truth only on rare occasions, just as it was an exception for Madeleine and Gustav to reveal the whole truth to their own children, just as their grandparents had kept the truth from their children and every generation from all subsequent generations, no matter whether the truths were vitally important or utterly trivial.

Again the cell phone rang—that little device which has kept everyone in constant touch with everyone else since the beginning of the last decade of the twentieth century, so that no one can claim the freedom of a hidden existence, even for a few hours.

"Where are you?" asked Amadée.

"We'll be there soon."

"But where are you exactly, right now?"

"On a bridge you don't know."

"How come I don't know it?"

"Because we've never driven over it, Amadée, that's how come."

"What's it called? Tell me what it's called and I can look in up on the Internet and see if there's a webcam there. Then you can wave to me and I'll see you!"

"Tappan Zee."

"Chimpanzee? And how come you're driving that way this time?"

"Because I made a wrong turn—but now everything's fine again."

"Hurry up. Mommy's so nervous. I can't stand her when she's like this."

"I'm hurrying. Promise. Kisses."

"Kisses, Dad."

"Could you ask Mommy if I should pick something up at the supermarket?"

"She'll call you back if she needs anything. Bye, Dad."

"Bye, Amadée."

He'd turned nine two weeks ago. Gustav's son didn't look like his father, and nothing about him reminded Gustav of his own childhood, neither his appearance nor the way he moved, neither his interests nor his roguish, uninhibited manners. His little daughter was much less a mystery than his son. She had something familiar in her eyes, something that reminded him of Ludwig. At her birth, right after she'd been lifted out of the cesarean incision, he was surprised by the similarity between her head and that of her grandfather, Ludwig Rubin, who had passed away six months earlier. Wolfgang Amadée, on the other hand, obviously had more of his mother's family. Madeleine's mother, who had been born in Tunisia and now lived in Marseilles, had a mouth curved very much like her grandson's, and the cut and darkness of Amadée's eyes were also more like his maternal grandmother than the rest of the family.

The vehicles around them gave the impression of being empty of people. They stood side by side, immobile, silent. No one honked, no one tried to break out of the mass of metal. One felt imprisoned, unable to move forward or backward. As soon as Gustav thought of leaving the car for just a moment, the lava flow suddenly crept forward again, but without making any significant progress—little more than thirty yards in fifteen minutes.

His father's ugly feet, the injured toenail on his left foot—Gustav couldn't free himself from the sensation of it. At the same time, he felt a strong and increasing need to pee. Where could you find a toilet here on the approach to the bridge?

His father's socks—they always had holes in them. All his socks had holes, especially the ones he wore on his left foot, the one with the yellowish, blackish toe. No pair of newly purchased socks stayed intact longer than three days. Usually he wore two unmatched socks, but when Gustav pointed this

out to him, he blamed Rosa. "Your mother put out two different socks for me again this morning! Look at the socks your
mother gives me . . ."

Father's white undershirts always had holes, too, where
they covered his belly. He was plagued by chronic gastritis his
whole life. When he was thirteen, as a test of courage in a Berlin
schoolyard, he had drunk an entire bottle of vinegar. They
pumped his stomach out at the Wilhelminenspital on Fehr-
belliner Platz. But the mucous membranes remained permanently
irritated. In restaurants he always ordered salads with no vinegar; often they forgot or didn't pay attention to his request. If
even the slightest smell of vinegar reached his nose, he sent the
plate back immediately. But his stomach was delicate in general, not just with respect to the feared vinegar. Father's bellowing
voice in the dimly lit restaurant of the Regina Hotel in Vienna;
they ate lunch there from time to time, on rainy Sundays or on
holidays, not least as an inner obeisance to Sigmund Freud, who
had been a regular at the Regina, his practice in the Berggasse
being no more than two minutes away on foot. Ludwig Rubin's
bellowing voice, one Sunday. He had ordered char, and when
the plate was put in front of him, he was surprised at how small
the portion was. His large nose sniffed the food. He wrinkled
it, made a face, and called the waiter over in a very loud voice,
since the fish didn't seem to be very fresh. As soon as the uni-
formed fellow stood before him, Father started yelling at him:
"How can such a tiny fish stink so much?!" The way Father
treated waiters in general! His son slid below the edge of the
table in embarrassment. Whenever Ludwig was in the midst of
ordering and the waitress or head waiter, the maitre d' or his

support staff didn't treat him with courtesy, he invariably added the remark, "And a side order of friendliness, if you please!" By contrast, Rosa was often satisfied as long as the restaurant plates were "really hot" and the establishment supplied its patrons with freshly laundered and ironed cloth napkins. She only lost her patience if the dishes had cooled off by the time they arrived at the table. She couldn't imagine any greater offense, called immediately for the owner or the manager of the place, and complained vehemently. (They almost always ate in restaurants, for neither Mother nor Father was capable of cooking. They invariably ruined even scrambled eggs. Their apartment, moreover, was in a permanent state of disarray, especially the kitchen, stuffed to the ceiling and more like an attic or a storage room one hasn't visited for decades than a place where food gets prepared.)

Gustav's parents were the kind of people who sent for the manager or asked to speak to the head of the establishment if they had the slightest complaint: in restaurants, in hotels, when they checked in at the airport, at the ticket window in train stations. They were the kind who always demand, never take no for an answer, who are persistent, insist on their rights, won't let go. They want special treatment for themselves, whether it's in a sleeping car, on a plane, or at a department store cash register. They always arrive late, whether for the theater or a concert, for an opera or a movie. They're even late for weddings and funerals. Everywhere, people have to stand up to let them by.

"Unfortunately, I need to go to the bathroom," he heard Mother say.

"So do I."

"What good does that do me, my darling?"

"We'll have to wait until we get to the other side."

"Don't hold your breath. It will take an hour at this rate. I certainly can't wait that long."

The oncoming lanes were strangely empty and looked as if they'd been stripped to the bone. The bulldozers had halted their work. Since the two traffic directions were separated by concrete barriers, you couldn't pull out into the oncoming lanes and turn back. Behind them, traffic was piling up steadily, which meant there was no possibility of turning around at the west end of the bridge, either. Hundreds were stuck—perhaps as many as a thousand cars were now at a standstill.

"Look! That red-and-white Oldsmobile up there has a forty-four on its license plate! And that one over there, too. What kind is it, that hideous yellow car? It has a forty-four on its plate, too!" As soon as Rosa caught sight of the number forty-four, she felt safe, no longer abandoned by fate. To her mind, the number forty-four produced a kind of pattern that gave her support. In her first years in Manhattan, she lived at 44 West 44th Street. She had just escaped from Europe and was on her own for the first time in her life, far from her parents, at a time when she could not have known about their deportation and murder. "And it was the first time in my life I was really, really happy. I've loved the number forty-four ever since. And you should love it too, because you're my son, after all."

Following the headlines at four p.m., the local station, WSDN in Tarrytown on the east side of the river, reported that traffic

on the Tappan Zee Bridge was badly congested in both directions. The cause of the backup was not yet known, but their
traffic report would be constantly updated.

"Stop fiddling with the radio and leave it on that station,"
Mother ordered.

Gustav sensed Father's presence around him—he didn't
just see Ludwig's feet and toes in his mind's eye, he saw his
ankles too, with their thin blue veins, saw his shins, his legs
with gray and white hairs on their pale skin, his naked legs up
to his knees. I see your kneecaps, Father, thought Gustav, and
I see the backs of your knees. I see down to your brittle bones,
right down to the marrow.

"What are you thinking about?" Rosa Rubin asked her son.

"Father's legs."

"Funny you should say that. Just this minute I was seeing
Papa's feet, his shins, and both legs up to the knees."

A shiver ran across Gustav's shoulders and down his back.

"And now?" she asked. "What are you thinking about
now?"

"Now I see him lying there naked, like a corpse ready to
be washed."

"Me too. I see him clearly. But just a few seconds before
you said it."

He put the car in neutral. Set the parking brake. Looked
at Mother, and she looked at him.

All around them people were getting out of their cars, calling
encouragement to each other. It was much too hot to stay in
the car very long with the air-conditioning turned off. Many

people were now sitting on hoods warmed up by the sun and the motors.

Gustav opened the heavy door on his side.

"Where are you going?" called Mother.

"Nowhere."

He went to the edge of the bridge. Here the roadway was not that high above the Hudson. They were only about a hundred yards from the west bank.

Now, suddenly, more aggressive honking was to be heard on all sides, with cries and shouts: *Enougho'this! C'm'on! Let'sgetgoin'! Whatthehellisthisdammit? Whatthefuck'sgoin'on?*

5

He stood at the bridge railing, looked south, looked down at the river. When they built the Tappan Zee in 1955, they had chosen one of the widest places in the entire three hundred-mile length of the Hudson River. At the time, there was talk that payoffs had been involved in getting the bridge constructed at this particular spot.

Here, as on every large bridge, Gustav had the feeling of being transported into a floating, dreamlike state. Since his earliest childhood, he had experienced the crossing of mighty bridges as the form of locomotion closest to flying. All bridges—those in his hometowns of New York, Los Angeles, and Vienna, those he encountered while traveling or found pictured in

books, magazines, or snapshots, those he stood on and those
he only saw from a distance—they all caused a slight quicken-
ing of his pulse, grounded him in the here and now while giving him a presentiment of ineffable, intangible things.

Gustav's paternal grandfather (he had died eighteen years
before Gustav's birth) suffered from gephyrophobia, the fear
of bridges and crossing bridges. Crossing the Charles Bridge
in Prague, where Theodor Rubin grew up and spent half his
brief life, was from his point of view a daring undertaking and
cost him great nervous exertion. Whether he had to cross a
bridge in a foreign city, on a train, or riding in a car, he began
to tremble, broke into a sweat, and was fearful for the seconds
or minutes it took to reach the other side. Sometimes he was
so afraid he had to throw up. In Prague, he mostly stayed in
the Mala Strana, where his apartment was, and avoided the
other half of the Golden City, the other side of the Vltava. On
August 1, 1976, the fortieth anniversary of Grandfather's death,
the Reichsbrücke in Vienna collapsed. Crossed by approxi-
mately eighteen thousand cars, trucks, and buses per hour on
weekdays, the bridge was carrying exactly four vehicles at the
time of its collapse, Sunday morning at 4:43 a.m. One car
plunged into the river and its twenty-two-year-old driver was
killed. A Vienna city bus with no passengers also went into the
river. The driver clambered onto the roof and was rescued
without injury.

On every bridge, whether it was only a few yards or several
miles long, Gustav always felt the same urge he had felt as a boy,
to throw a piece of wood into the stream on one side and then

run over to the other to see it come shooting out and continue its journey, struggling to keep itself above water. For as long as they could, father and son would watch the fantasy vessel float away. Then they would look for another branch. Or make a boat of folded newspaper, drop it in, and repeat the process again and again and again. Whenever they set foot on a bridge together, they automatically began searching for a piece of wood, a plastic bottle, or a piece of cardboard they could christen an ocean liner, and that went on for as long as Father was alive. At forty, Gustav played the bridge game with his son Amadée with the same yearning he had felt at four and fourteen.

Leaning over the railing of the Tappan Zee, Gustav looked down at the foaming waters of the Hudson which had broken against the piers on the north side of the bridge, out of his sight, before emerging on the south side, churned up and rushing on toward New York City. He considered getting the mineral-water bottle out of the trunk. It would float on the waves. If he climbed over the concrete barriers dividing the two directions, he could throw it in on the north side, but by the time he got back to the south side, his ship probably would have long since bobbed out of sight.

Gustav looked down again, down to where the bridge piers emerged from the gurgling water.

And then, in that moment, he noticed it for the first time. He saw it as clearly as he saw all around him the dense jam of cars, trucks, buses, motorcycles, sailboats and motorboats on trailers, the overweight men in baseball caps, and the ever-growing number of children getting out of their cars. Down there, in the river, directly beneath and parallel to the Tappan Zee Bridge, lay the gigantic naked body of his father. Directly under him, at the western end of the bridge, the waters of the Hudson were washing in foaming waves over Father's feet. They lay as if anchored to one of the broad stone surfaces sticking out into the river at right angles to the piers. Father's head, however, lay more than a mile away, at the eastern end of the bridge, in the shallower water near the left bank of the Hudson. In between lay Father's legs, buttocks, and crotch, his slightly bloated belly, his arms, and his chest with the three nipples. Beneath his right nipple, he had a third, somewhat smaller one. Gustav had a tiny one in exactly the same place, and this reassured him, as he was growing up, that he wasn't an adopted child. You couldn't see it clearly from where Gustav was standing, Father's little nipple, only guess that it was there.

How could he be sure the figure down there was his father, resting stretched out on its left side—the heart side—and monumentally long?

He glimpsed shoulders in the distance, guessed at neck, goiter, chin, one cheek, thought he could spy a closed eye, saw a furrowed brow, a shock of thick white hair. The giant rested on its arm, pelvis, and thigh: motionless, but not lifeless; passed away, but not dead. Not a single sign of decomposition anywhere. Every wrinkle, every vein, the texture of the skin, the color of the hair—everything just as it had been when he was alive. No doubt about it, it was the fatherbody, lying there like Gulliver stranded in Lilliput. The father he had idolized, his best friend, his big brother, the fatheranimal that seemed to him immortal. Ludwig Rubin, who had assured him at regular intervals since he was a little boy, You'll see, Gustav my *boychick*, I'm going to live to be a hundred and twenty. You'll see!

He couldn't get his fill of the sight, and now felt his scalp prickle. He stared for long minutes down at the giant body of his father, suspended over the water on the footings of the piers. Down below, a further proof he no longer needed by now: the big toe with the yellowish-brownish-blackish nail, thick, misshapen, kaput, wide as a rock and quite clearly visible. Father! Dear Father! Such a tender, dear, affectionate, and gentle person as you (as long as you weren't having one of your violent, raging temper tantrums that turned you into a monster), your small, quite compact body, a bit pudgy even, stretched out over a mile? Can you hear me? Can you feel me near?

I must hurry way up there to your head, Father. I want to see if your eyes are open. I can't leave here right now: Mother's waiting for me. Forgive me; please have patience. I'll get up there to your forehead, your lips, your skull, as soon as I can, as quickly as ever I can. I promise.

He returned to the car. Mother must be told nothing—the incomprehensible event had to remain Gustav's innermost secret.

"I can't believe you left me here alone for so long . . ."

"Sorry, I felt a little strange all of a sudden . . ."

"You don't have to tell me, Burschi. I know all about it. If my bladder weren't so full, I'd take a look at it right now. I just can't at the moment."

"What are you talking about?"

"You're entering the twilight zone, reaching out to ghosts."

He stared at her. There was no way she could know what he had just seen.

"My Burschi is lying under the bridge," she whispered, "naked, stretched out on his back, or maybe on his side, the way he sleeps in bed . . ."

"Mom, you're hallucinating!"

"First of all, don't lie to me. And secondly, find me somewhere to go wee-wee, right now. Thirdly, they said on the radio there's a huge truck tipped over on its side, blocking all the lanes fairly far up ahead, at the eastern end of the bridge. It may take a long time. We should call Em."

"Madeleine. Or Mad. Her name isn't Em."

"Whatever. I need a bathroom."

Father was stretched out under the bridge, a mile long. How could Mother possibly know? Were they really having a conversation about finding a toilet, while the gigantic body of his father lay under the Tappan Zee? Gustav moved, spoke, thought, breathed as though everything was as it had always been, an ordinary Friday afternoon at the end of the twentieth century. Was he really arguing with his mother about what his wife's name was?

He ran back to the railing of the bridge and looked down into the waves. Father's feet, Father's monstrous legs, playfully lapped by the Hudson. They lay there unchanged, immobile, just as before. The first time he hadn't noticed the strands of algae wrapped around Father's toes.

Those feet, those legs so much more powerful than the son's. Father's feet always steered when they went sledding. It was always Ludwig who steered, never Gustav. The son was forbidden to steer as a child. He pleaded: let me steer! but Ludwig never allowed him to. How much more stamina Father had on their hiking tours through Scotland, Denmark, Holland, France, Yugoslavia, Italy. How much stronger his wanderlust in Brittany, on the Hungarian plains. How much more nimble his lusty uphill marches in Sicily, the Pyrenees, in South Tirol. The former track star who in his youth had won international hundred-meter, four-hundred-meter, one-kilometer races, strode through the landscape, often with Gustav trotting along far behind him. That's how they traveled through regions they'd never visited before. Only in exceptional circumstances did they hitchhike or ride buses or local trains. They always entrusted themselves to chance, let themselves drift. Father had conditioned Gustav to insecurity. He taught his son to venture into the world every day without certainty but also without fear. They'd find a roof over their heads before nightfall, you just had to surrender fearlessly to fate. The right path awaited them at every fork in the trail. Everything would turn out all right; it was foreordained. When Gustav was a boy, Father was so convinced of this that the adolescent adopted the same attitude toward life. However strewn with obstacles the path, have confidence! Everything will turn out fine. And if not fine, then surely as it was meant to be. Accept chance events as things that fall to your lot of necessity. Have trust in the pattern of your life: everything happens as it's supposed to happen. Feel safe in the heart of the flux of reality. Father had drummed it into his son: You must not give up! Again and again that single sentence: Never give up in life! No matter what may happen to you, don't give up! (Only in the final years of his life did his confidence turn into its opposite. Then it was the son who reassured the father: Don't worry! We'll find a roof over our heads. The father hesitated, seemed a bit fearful, couldn't believe everything would turn out all right.)

It was as if twenty, thirty, forty years after the end of the war, they were both reliving the emigration. And before they went to sleep Father told his son stories from his life. On their hiking tours he readily divulged his exploits in Prague, Berlin, Vienna, New York, and California: the stations of his emigration, postwar incidents, amorous adventures. And Gustav was addicted to Ludwig's reminiscences, couldn't get enough of his father's retrospection, drove him further and further into the past until they both fell asleep, simultaneously, in midsentence.

Gustav never regarded as unpleasant this trotting along behind his father—not just when they were on hikes but also when they entered restaurants, cafés, railway compartments. His inferiority seemed a natural state and he accepted it. Head held high, father strode ahead; two or three yards behind came his stooping son. And once they were finally seated, Father became absorbed in the seven, eight, nine daily papers in three or four languages he always carried around with him, rattled them loudly while tearing out articles he thought he needed to save for later. Not infrequently, he then forgot them when he left the restaurant, room, train, plane. Gustav reminded Father of them, but sometimes failed to do so, and then whatever he had torn out to save was, as a rule, lost. Or Gustav deliberately neglected to remind Ludwig to gather up his belongings, and then he felt a certain satisfaction at the sight of his father's distraught expression. I've lost those articles I tore out! I've misplaced my glasses! Where's that package of books that came in the mail this morning? Did I leave it on the table in the coffeehouse? This little pleasure, however, was often overshadowed by the need to return to the place where they had just been in order to recover the items, an assignment that often fell to Gustav, not just in his youth, but on into his adulthood—basically up until Father's death. He often returned with bad news: they threw away the plastic bag with your clippings right after we left and couldn't find it again. I asked the waiter to look through the trash, but unfortunately, no luck. Even a hefty tip didn't help. Your hat (your umbrella, your wallet) has also vanished without a trace.

"You could fill a string of boxcars with the things I've lost in my life!" Father would then always groan. "Caps, glasses, coats, sweaters, fountain pens, ballpoints, three typewriters. Watches even, top-shelf, insanely expensive wristwatches. And a thousand other things . . ."

When father and son walked their weekly circuit together in the cities where Ludwig lived—New York, Los Angeles, and Vienna—Gustav walked alongside him rather than trotting behind. These circuits had begun when Gustav was ten or eleven and remained the rule into Father's final years. They met on Saturday afternoons and always completed the same course around a large area of the city, following the same alleys and streets. The most important principle was circularity, to avoid returning along the same route.

The son walked bent forward—leaning like a stalk of bamboo in a storm, his hands clasped behind him and resting on his tailbone, casting sidelong glances at his father, who was a head shorter than he. On these walks, father and son related and exchanged and discussed what each had thought, done, and neglected to do during the past week. As a rule, Ludwig had more to say than his son. He talked about his trips to give lectures, attend conferences, do research, about his train trips from one provincial town to the next, journeys which haunted and tortured Gustav's dreams although they were Father's journeys: late trains, missed connecting flights, dining cars, sleeping cars, coaches with couchettes, local trains, terminals, unpacking, packing, emptying suitcases, repacking suitcases, purchasing in foreign cities what had been left behind at home: forgotten shoes, shirts, pajamas, pants, underwear, and toilet articles of all kinds.

The son spoke of uneventful activity, his historical research, his endeavor to pursue every aspect of the Hundred Years War, however peripheral it might be. For his father, he brought alive moments from the fourteenth century that seemed so timeless, so modern that Richard II and Charles VI might have been living in the present. Later, he told Father about the peculiarities of the profession he had embarked upon against Ludwig's will, things that must always have sounded incomprehensible to him: auctions in Toronto, Hong Kong, and Copenhagen, in Helsinki and Stockholm, farm stocks in Russia, North America, and Southeast Asia, the introduction of new slaughtering techniques that caused the fur-bearing animals a bit less suffering.

A powerful west wind was blowing across the Tappan Zee. Drivers stopped honking; there was no more point to it. By now the jam had become so dense, the collection of stranded cars so hopelessly impermeable, that forward progress was unthinkable. People stood around in large groups talking about the situation. Everyone was surprised that neither police sirens nor the clatter of helicopters was to be heard. Gustav watched a woman with long blond hair staring straight ahead with her mouth open, tears running in little rivulets down her reddened cheeks. People were playing cards on the hoods of their cars, unpacking sandwiches. Others got out their video cameras, filmed each other and the motionless scene. They shot everything around them. To Gustav's relief, however, it didn't occur to any of them to point their cameras down toward the river, toward the bridge piers, down where the fatherbody lay.

In a windowless trailer, cows, calves, and pigs were mooing and squealing for all they were worth. There was no visible ventilation and the driver sat in his cab, immobile, as if frozen in the midsummer heat.

"You have to look for a motor home, Burschi. It's my only hope," Mother called to her son through the open window. "And hurry! Stop looking under the bridge for now, at least until my problem is solved. One thing at a time . . ."

He scouted around for an RV, passed children throwing a lurid yellow plastic ball back and forth, again and again, over the roofs of several cars.

In a tiny car a small wirehaired dachshund was barking. The windows were closed tight. It had been abandoned by its owners, was suffering from the heat, its tongue lolling out. The little dog looked very much like the one from an apartment house at the edge of the vineyards in Grinzing that Gustav often played with when he was six or seven years old. Mucki belonged to the concierge and his wife, who lived on the ground floor. Gustav was quite fond of the animal and one evening before going to bed, informed his father (who had very little time for him back then), "I love Mucki much more than you!" Deeply hurt, Ludwig said nothing. Gustav never repeated this remark.

No sooner was her son out of sight than Mother very quickly went over to the railing and cast a first look down onto the resurrected body of her deceased husband. When she saw him lying there like that, she burst into tears. A frail gentleman stopped beside her. He was older than Mother, but he steadied her with his arm. "Can I help you?" he asked. "Anything the matter?"

She thanked him—and, for a change, remained utterly silent.

6

High above Father's shins, Gustav was moving in the direction of his kneecaps and looking down every twenty-five yards. At every lamppost, he stopped and looked down. His heart hadn't beaten so rapidly and irregularly for years, not since before his operation. He came up to a motor home, quite roomy and completely colorless. The white lace curtains were drawn shut around its entire perimeter.

He knocked on the passenger-side door. No answer. Had the occupants left? He looked around, trying to guess who they might be. "Yeah?" came a sonorous male voice from inside the vehicle. "Whaddayawant?!" Gustav apologized for the disturbance, but the rear door was already opening. An elderly gentleman emerged, very thin and with a large, pointed nose. His hair, partly white and partly yellowish, was plastered stickily to his head. "Whaddayawant?!" he repeated. One lens of his glasses had a crack in it. Gustav took note of the blue plastic raincoat the man was wearing despite the oppressive summer heat, and beneath that he could make out a dark gray suit with lighter pinstripes, a vest of saturated bottle green with lots of beautiful mother-of-pearl buttons, and a snow-white shirt.

"So? What is it?" the man repeated his question, somewhat less gruffly this time. Gustav thought he detected a slight accent and asked if German was his native language. The old man shook himself as if all German speakers were subhuman. His father was from Strasbourg and his mother had been a "woman from Vienna," he replied, "a *Weanerin*, as they say in Austria. And my sister has a café in Vienna, Café Schubert it's called, right near the giant Ferris wheel in the Wurstelprater. But that certainly doesn't mean I either like, care for, or ever speak the German language!"

"My mother is from Vienna too, born and raised there!" Gustav intended to follow up on this remark by immediately asking if Rosa could use the toilet.

"I don't want to speak German. Didn't you get it? I do not like speaking German. Don't ask me to speak German again, will you? I'm not too sad about this delay," the owner of the motor home continued before Gustav was able to ask his question. "The longer a trip in my motor home lasts, the better. I think the airplane is mankind's most horrific invention. It's only since we've had airplanes that wars have turned into worldwide orgies of destruction. Without the airplane things would be better on earth!" He shook himself, lurched, reached out his huge hands like wings, flapped his arms. "No, anything but flying! I travel through the States in my motor home, but in Europe I take the train, since I can travel all over Europe by train for nothing. You see, I used to work for the railway. I was the stationmaster of Victoria Station in London."

"Sorry to interrupt you," Gustav tried again. "May I ask you a favor—"

"You may, of course you may. I really was the stationmaster of one of the largest train stations in the world from 1947 to 1988. That's forty-one years, all told. Are you familiar with Victoria Station in London? But I like to use the railroad system in the USA too. I once crossed thirty-seven states from east to west on a single trip! I swear I did! On the life of my sister! No two ways about it. Where was I?"

"We have the following problem, if I might interrupt you for a moment, my mother is an elderly woman and really has to—"

"It's so nice to talk to you! It's really a pleasure. So, as I was saying, the only time in my life I flew, it was utterly atrocious! The takeoff was just tolerable, and even the flight itself was halfway OK, but the landing was absolutely unbearable!" His winglike hands shot out and his body wobbled like a wide-bodied jet getting ready to land in a storm. "The landing!" he repeated.

Instead of at last conveying Mother's request, Gustav now uttered the words, "I often arrived at Victoria Station with my parents." His eyes fell on a wide, unmade bed inside the vehicle, cooking facilities, and a dining table covered with a white plastic tablecloth. On it, a half-empty gin bottle. The floor was a big mess: shirts, pants, socks were lying about among newspapers, magazines, toilet paper. "Because when we traveled from Vienna to London to visit the Wasserstein brothers (they were my mother's closest childhood friends and had a shop for antiquarian German books), we always traveled by train. Mother had a terrible fear of flying, so we took the sleeper to Ostend and crossed over by ship. The boat was like a giant bridge across the channel."

"The train from Vienna always arrived on platform two," continued the stationmaster happily, "and the taxicabs would drive right up alongside the train. You could climb directly from your sleeping car into a cab, you remember? I mourn for the days when trains still made it possible to travel in luxury! The only other place luxury travel was available was on ocean liners, which have almost completely died out too. And I must add—for the record, so to speak—that in a few years there won't be any sleeping cars left either. I can feel it, I can sense it. Just like there aren't any luggage nets left today. How I loved those nets! They disappeared in the mid-Sixties. There's no longer a single train anywhere in Europe with luggage nets; they've all got those ghastly rigid metal racks. I must tell you, when I was still a lad, those luggage nets were the most beautiful thing in the world. Did they still have them when you were small? I can hardly describe what blissful joy it was to enter a compartment with my parents and have it all to ourselves. We pulled the curtains closed on the corridor side, spread ourselves out, the three of us—Father, Mother, and I—and really cluttered it up on purpose, got everything out of our bags—clothes, food, books, medicine bottles—so that no one dared to come into our compartment, except for the conductor, of course. We scared away every intruder. And no sooner had we gotten under way than I scrambled up into that soft luggage net. I did it until I was sixteen, seventeen, eighteen even! What a feeling! The view from up there, right under the domed ceiling of the car, down onto the heads of my beloved parents and out onto the rails, out onto the passing fields—"

"If I could just ask a quick question—" Gustav desperately interjected.

"You'd rather hear more about my experiences on the big ocean liners, wouldn't you? My most terrific crossing was on the *France*. My God, that was a huge ship, one of the most beautiful ever! I was on its last voyage in 1973. Just as we were about to dock in Le Havre after six days at sea, the longshoremen went on strike. We couldn't disembark. The ship's crew were in solidarity with the dock workers, and all the passengers who didn't absolutely need or want to disembark were allowed to remain on board. I lived in the lap of luxury for ten days. The personnel got the best food out of the deep freezers and thawed it out, and of course they opened the very best wines. It was sensational. You've got to remember that the *France* employed one hundred eighty-eight cooks."

"My father often traveled on the *France*, and so have I. There's even a photo of me in the dining room." Gustav thought he needed to draw more attention to himself; it was his only chance to finally get in his bathroom request.

But the old man continued unflappably. "I have a strong connection to chefs. You see, my father was a well-known chef in prewar Vienna. He worked in high-class hotels—the Imperial and the Carlton. You'd have a hard time imagining how devoted I was to my father, young man, even when I was twenty. Young people today have almost nothing to say to their fathers, isn't that so? But then the war came. He got drafted immediately, right at the beginning of the Polish campaign, and I was sent to the eastern front. You can't even go to the bathroom anymore, I can tell you that. You just completely forget how to piss and shit. My mate had his head blown off right next to me, right in front of my eyes. And all on account of the policies of a madman and because another madman, namely Stalin, opposed him. I've had it with bloodbaths—up to my nipples! If epochs could give themselves the deathblow, this century would have opted for suicide."

The owner of the motor home gave himself a silent shake, his shoulders rose and fell in a rapid rhythm, as if he were laughing. Or crying?

"Apropos toilet, my mother has really got to go—"

"Absolutely not! If I let your mother use my chemical toilet, hordes of people would be knocking at my door and asking for the same favor as you." His voice took on a whiny, tormented quality. "I've been terrified somebody would ask me that, ever since this backup started. That's why I was so relieved to find such a cultivated person as yourself at my door, someone who wasn't looking for any favors at all. Forget it. My answer is final. It's not going to happen!"

Suddenly, there was Mother facing the man. "Thank you. You're a good person," she whispered. She clambered up the three steps into his motor home, right in front of his nose, opened a narrow door, and locked it from inside.

Taken completely off guard, the man hissed, "What gall! What unbelievable nerve!"

Gustav asked his forgiveness, thanked him effusively, but it didn't help.

"There are limits—and you two have crossed them," the man growled. "I was ambushed!"

Gustav fished a ten-dollar bill out of his pocket.

"Absolutely not. It's a matter of principle. I admit we've gotten to know each other a bit, you and I, but that has nothing to do with it."

You could hear the toilet flushing. Mother emerged and smiled like an Olympic gold medal winner. "Many, many thanks. My son has to go too. Is that all right?"

"Come on, Mother. This gentleman is already quite angry with us . . ." He pulled at the sleeve of Rosa's jacket. "Let's go!"

"But—you can't wait any longer either, can you?! By the way, sir, you look uncannily like my old tutor in mathematics, the famous philosopher Karl Popper. But he died five years ago. Has anybody ever told you that before? Are you Jewish?"

The former stationmaster of Victoria Station slammed the door on them.

Some distance up ahead, the eastbound traffic seemed to be thinning out and moving forward now. The drivers all jumped into their cars and started their engines at the same time. Mother and son ran—as fast as it was possible for Rosa to run—back to the Cadillac. They'd left the cell phone on the seat, and it was vibrating as they got in. Gustav turned on the ignition.

Mother talked to Madeleine, cautiously breaking the news that there would be an additional delay, while their car rolled forward ten or twelve yards, in rhythm with all the other vehicles around them.

They could clearly hear Mad burst into tears. "Please give her to me!" Gustav reached over to take the telephone.

"She doesn't want to talk to you. She says she can't take it anymore. Should I tell her about Father?"

Gustav vehemently shook his head. He feared it would only be one more—unnecessary—strain on her sensitive nerves.

"No, Em, nothing about Father, nothing. We'll call you again as soon as we have more details." She turned off the cell phone. "I would have gone ahead and told her, but it's up to you. You're married to her, not me. I think it's wonderful, this thing with Father. There's nothing oppressive or frightening about it."

They came to a standstill again. They were not far from the place where the midsection of the Tappan Zee Bridge rises to its highest elevation. Gustav thought he could make out a camera on top of the structure, installed up there next to a small American flag to monitor the flow of traffic. He got out of the car, waved in the direction of the girders, waved for a long time, got back behind the wheel.

"What was that all about?" Mother asked.

"You should wave too. Amadée can probably see us on his computer at home."

"How's that?"

"Do you know what a webcam is?"

Mother shook her head. "What kind of thing is it? What's it got to do with my grandson?"

He was too tired to explain to her how it was possible for Amadée to be observing the bridge.

"Does that mean he could see Ludwig?"

"The camera only sees the deck of the bridge, not what's going on underneath it."

"Thank God! Otherwise people all over the world could . . . see Papa lying down there."

"So you do know what a webcam is?"

"Can't you leave me alone, Gustav? Please?"

The local station reported that the cleanup operation would in all likelihood go on into the early evening hours. In the meantime, they had learned that the overturned tractor-trailer had been transporting toluene, a colorless distillate of petroleum and coal used in the manufacture of saccharin. It was also one of the ingredients in hair coloring and was used in photography and the pharmaceutical industry. Some drivers in the immediate vicinity of the accident had been transported to the hospital emergency room in Tarrytown with possible chemical poisoning. Toluene could cause numbness and, through direct contact, irritation of the mucous membranes. There was no cause for panic.

The wind was blowing from west to east, carrying the fumes away from mother and son.

"No cause for panic?" Rosa repeated in indignation. "I always get the most terrible headaches and dizzy spells from stuff like that."

"Toluene? . . . Never heard of it."

"There's not much you do know. I've often been struck by the fact that you're pretty ignorant, especially when it comes to practical things. You were always slow on the uptake, in all areas. What other eleven-year-old would still get other people to spread butter and honey on his bread for him? But now I'd like to finally take a look at Father. I didn't want to earlier, not when my bladder was full. Come on and show him to me. Then this madness you've caused us here with your typical getting lost will at least have made some sense."

Mother was acting as if she hadn't already long since gone over to the edge of the bridge and looked down. For no reason at all, she wasn't telling the truth. That's how it had always been.

"Haven't you taken a look yet at all? I can hardly believe that," Gustav continued the game.

"Me? With a full bladder? Never! You know how I am."

On the radio Maria Callas in the role of Elizabeth de Valois was singing an aria from Verdi's *Don Carlos*. "Turn that off! She's just yowling!" Whenever Father heard a high voice singing on the radio, he immediately cried out, "She's just yowling!"

When the radio was turned off, they got out and squeezed past the hoods, fenders, and bumpers in the direction of the railing. He felt a certain reluctance to look down again. On the one hand, he feared Father wouldn't be lying down there anymore. On the other hand, he was afraid Father was still very much down there, just as before.

Rosa took the decision out of his hands. "Let me do it alone, please," she called to him. "I don't want you with me when I look down."

He turned back, opened the trunk, looked in his carry-on bag for the bottle of water he had bought in Reykjavik. The bottle was half empty. He poured what was left onto the road and crawled into the trunk. With his head deep in the interior, his legs still stuck halfway out. He rolled onto his side and pulled his legs into the fetal position, opened his fly, and peed into the plastic bottle. Felt the warmth of the urine radiating through the thin plastic to the palm of his hand.

What an easy time of it we men have! Father often said. He always took an empty hot-water bottle with him on his train trips. Instead of having to climb down from his bunk in the middle of the night and run from his compartment to the toilet at the end of the corridor, or pee into the porcelain bowl under the washstand, he preferred to use the pissbottle, as he called it. Don't forget to pack my pissbottle! he would call to his family through the apartments of Gustav's childhood. And do I still have fresh poopies? Poopies—those were the balls of wax he pressed deep into his ears, little pink spheres from the Oropax company which were, of course, indispensable for over-night train trips.

Gustav screwed the cap back on the plastic bottle, stowed it in the farthest corner of the trunk, and unfolded himself from his hiding place while a small group of people stood watching. They guessed what he had been doing in the trunk. A muscular fellow with bare, tanned arms laughed out loud, said he'd had the same idea. It was probably the only alternative to standing on the edge of the bridge and aiming your stream down into the river. Gustav nodded in silence. It terrified him to imagine that from now on all the men and boys the whole length of the bridge might relieve themselves onto Ludwig Rubin's body.

Mother returned, ashen-faced, from the edge of the bridge. "Very, very strange business. It seems a bit fishy to me. There was quite an attractive young woman standing nearby and I asked her . . . to . . . to look down and tell me what she saw. Because I thought, maybe I've gone meshugge and Burschi and I are just imagining things that aren't there. But then she stared at me, very agitated, and ran away—quite fast, in fact, as if she had seen a ghost. She was really very upset."

7

Father had died eleven months ago, after a year of unremitting, round-the-clock torment. A year lying almost motionless on his back, ringing for help, calling four, five times an hour, begging: please fix my pillows, please lay, maneuver, shove me back into a more comfortable position. He'd suffered a stroke that hit him with the impact of a guillotine. For the first three weeks, he couldn't get out a single word. And once he was able to communicate again, struggling over every syllable, he commanded his wife and his son to hand him back his right leg, which was lying over there on the next bed. Gustav informed him that his leg was still attached to his body, just as it had always been. That simply made him madder.

"No," he growled, "I can see it lying right over there! Give it back to me! Fasten it back onto my body, I can't live with only one leg and just leave the other leg lying over there on the next bed!"

To distract him, Gustav talked about the game they had played so often in years gone by. It was called the children store. In every large city there were shops offering children for sale. You had a trial period, and if you were not satisfied with a boy or girl because they were badly behaved, ugly, stupid, or for any other reason, you could pay a small surcharge and exchange the child you had bought for a new one. And if you were still not happy, even with this new child, you had a last chance to exchange the replacement girl or boy, but then for a very steep additional charge. On their hikes, on their city walks, before going to sleep, or after they got up on Sunday mornings, father and son would envision these orgies of shopping and exchanging in great detail. Many of the branch offices featured a body parts department, where they would repair or replace injured arms, legs, eyes, noses, hands, and feet. You could get a look at the newest models and try them out on your child's body. All of this cost a lot of money, of course, but there were always plenty of customers who patronized these children stores to supply themselves with offspring.

Father lay still, and with the help of his right hand, tried to comprehend the left hand paralyzed by the stroke. He petted his left hand with his right. He stroked it as if it were a kitten purring in his lap. On every visit, Gustav endeavored to make conversation. "Beloved Father!" he called in greeting. "Beloved son," Ludwig groaned in a deep voice, a voice that wasn't at all his own. Gustav had more and more trouble thinking of sentences he could say to his father, topics to discuss, things to report. Even telling him the world news or reading aloud from nonfiction works that Ludwig's ravenous curiosity would have earlier skimmed in a single day, elicited no reaction at all from him. He lay there or sat, motionless, in a wheelchair, and stared silently into the distance, then often closed his eyes. The last words he said to Gustav—one had to strain to understand him, his words were slurred, he had to search for each letter, grope for consonants, for vowels—his last sentence was "Son, my boy, beloved Burschi, tell Mommy to stop dominating me so much all the time. It never lets up, never lets up."

They buried him next to his mother in the cemetery on Staten Island, New York, which the son had visited with his father once years before. It was 103 degrees in the shade and they couldn't find Gustav's grandmother's grave. Ludwig couldn't remember where he'd buried his mother. Dripping with perspiration, they returned to the cemetery entrance. They asked to see the registry. Under December 8, 1948, they discovered the row and grave number. They found the grave, overgrown with weeds. They could barely still read the name Selly Branden Rubin. No one had been here since the burial. This was Father's first and only visit to his mother's grave in four decades. Ten years before it would become his own gravesite, he had laid a small pebble on the stela.

For eleven months, Gustav Robert Rubin said Kaddish for Ludwig David Rubin, who was in the habit of characterizing his son's religious commitment as a return to the Middle Ages. "Ever heard of the Enlightenment? You of all people, Gustav. As a historian, you must recognize your turn to piety as a betrayal of the ideals of your forefathers who were liberated from the yoke of belief! Do me a favor, please don't get too observant, I beg you!"

Three times a day for eleven months, he said the words *Yit'gadal v'yit'kadash sh'mei raba, b'al'ma di v'ra khir'utei v'yam'likh mal'khutei b'chayeikhon uv'yomeikhon uv'chayei d'khol beit Yis'ra'eil, ba'agala uviz'man kariv. V'm'ru: Amein!* "May His great Name grow exalted and sanctified in the world that He created as He willed. May He give reign to His kingship in your lifetimes and in your days, and in the lifetimes of the entire Family of Israel, swiftly and soon. Now say: Amen!"

It is written in the books of the Law, in the Talmud, in the Shulchan Arukh, that even the basest of souls need at most eleven months, not twelve, to be washed clean of their sins and escape hell. A few days before his departure from Vienna, the eleven months of Kaddish had come to an end, and in a small prayer room in the Grünangergasse, in the presence of Lichtmann and eight other men, Gustav had spoken the prayer for the dead for his father one last time.

My past is of no interest to me. Father repeated his credo at every opportunity: I look ahead, always forward, only forward. I think of the present moment and I think of the future, not of what's happened, not of yesterday's events. If some day after my hundred and twentieth birthday I might not be around anymore, then don't look for me in a cemetery—God forbid!

(in whom I don't believe). Visit me at the stream that falls into the valley at Tarasp instead, up in the forest, where we built that dam when you were eleven years old. We slaved away there every summer until you were thirteen. Or seek me where we hiked on our annual tours. Go to the spots in the forests where we built campfires, in the Engadine, in Umbria, in the foothills of the Pyrenees. Look for me where we roasted potatoes and then peeled off their crusty, sooty skins, where we burned our fingertips to eat them. How they steamed! Look for me where we hunted and found blueberries, mushrooms, and wild strawberries—they were my favorites, the strawberries were. We always called them *strong* because they gave us the strength to go on. You're more likely to find me in any of the places I just named than in a graveyard.

And just a few weeks after Father's death, Gustav did look for Ludwig at that stream above the village of Tarasp in the lower Engadine. For three summers they had worked to create a harbor: a large, wide pool in which to anchor little wooden ships and folded paper boats. To do so, they had to tame a whole section of the stream, and arrest the wild, precipitous rush of the water into the valley by means of several yard-high dams. They had lugged heavy stones, shoved medium-sized boulders, slaved away every day of school vacation. And they succeeded. Slowly, they had created a pool, built their harbor. The stone dams held. On the next-to-last day of their third summer in Tarasp, they were able to launch their little armada of homemade boats for the first time. They let them shoot thirty or forty yards down glassy clear rapids, and watched as the miniature barks and barges, paper gondolas and cigarette packages reached the anchorage through the bubbling white foam of the harbor they had dug out, as if steered by ghostly hands, and sidled up to the shores of the bays Gustav and Father had created in hours of happy labor. So now, on a narrow, steep forest path which, as Gustav thought, led to this spot, he stumbled, slid down into the streambed, crossed to the other bank on rocks that formed a stony ford and continued climbing as the path grew steeper.

All of a sudden, a gigantic stag was standing before Gustav —high, wide, and mighty, a ten-pointer who didn't take flight but instead licked his black muzzle with his big tongue and seemed to be smiling. The stag stood still, rooted to the spot on his powerful legs, his antlered head slightly lowered, but in greeting rather than getting ready to charge. And so they remained, son and stag, tête-à-tête, face-to-face, the man motionless, the animal motionless, a whole minute long. And then the stag turned away from Gustav and climbed unhurriedly up the steep hillside.

Three months after Father's death, his son tried again to force a meeting, this time along hiking paths near the town of San Gimignano. He marched along where they had once wandered through the Tuscan vineyards when he was twelve years old— Father on his powerful legs, his weary son trotting along behind. Father Quixote, son Panza. They never knew until late afternoon where they would spend the night. Everything was left to chance. And they always found a roof over their heads, with a farmer or in someone's little house at the edge of a village.

He sought him there, but didn't find him. No sign, no omen. Or was there? He found his way back to Certaldo, the home of the medieval poet Boccaccio.

Back then, not far from the market town of Certaldo, they had plucked grapes from the vines. It was a very hot day in September, the dark blue grapes ripe and sweet, warm from the sun. They stole more and more of the fruit, the taste of their booty more and more intoxicating. Then they heard a man give a wild shout. The stranger approached them swiftly, leaping down the hill like a billy goat. He was unshaven, unkempt, his clothes covered with dirt. He ran toward them, gesticulating and shouting. Father whispered in fright, "It's the farmer who owns this vineyard." And when the man was just a few steps away from them, Ludwig gave his son a hard slap as punishment for the theft they had committed together. Before Gustav had time to burst into tears, he heard the farmer lamenting, "No! No! No!" And Father begged the vineyard owner's pardon. He could speak Italian well, at least well enough to express his regret effectively.

The farmer was beside himself. No, not because of the theft of this crop, not at all, on the contrary, he was beside himself that the father had slapped his son. "Take them! Take as many as you like! That's why I was calling to you. You misunderstood me. Please, take as many as you want." And he invited the two of them to his house, at the top of the vineyard. Signor Casertini lived there with his wife and four children. They stayed for dinner, a chicken roasted in fresh rosemary sprigs, and drank the farmer's wine. Gustav drank some too, even though he was still a child. They stayed the night in a soft double bed in a back room of the farmhouse, with a picture of the Virgin hanging above it. Father, however, never apologized to Gustav for slapping him.

"Come on, let's look down together this time," Rosa suggested, awakening him from his trance.

They threaded their way through the cars and groups of people.

"Did you notice how they're all lower class—every last one of them?" Mother complained.

"How can you tell?"

"I can tell, that's all. I just can. It's disgusting. They're all eating with their hands, out of paper bags. Their fingers dripping with mayonnaise. Not a workingman in sight—because workers have something dignified about them, even in America —and I don't see any intellectuals, either, and almost no children or animals."

"I saw a few children earlier, Mother, and you heard the mooing cattle and squealing pigs yourself . . ."

"Just wretched, ugly, lower-class people . . . God, how I hate them!"

"And what about that stretch limo? Don't you wonder who's in there?"

"Another petit bourgeois, I bet you!"

Gustav caught his pants on a bent fender, ripped open the lower part of the left pant leg, but he didn't mention the mishap to Rosa. She would only start carrying on and scolding him.

"Did you go wee-wee somewhere already?" she asked.

"Mother, I'm forty-five years old. Don't you think I'm old enough to take care of these things myself?"

"Don't argue with me, Burschi. Father's listening. When something this incredible is happening to us, you mustn't criticize me. A really big miracle is happening to the two of us and you're reprimanding me? I'm still very confused by what we're going through, at least as much as you are! Let's make peace. Both of us. Be nice to me. Or a little nicer, at least."

They stood by the bridge railing and looked down at the Hudson. There he lay, monster, fallen angel, handsome man, the living dead, deceased fountain of life. The New York undertaker had already shut Ludwig's small, ritually washed body into its simple casket by the time Gustav arrived, a day after Ludwig's death. Just before the burial, the wooden box lay on trestles in a dirty cemetery shed among tattered prayer books and rusting garden tools. The muddy ground was covered with footprints. Next to the casket was a gray stone slab for washing the bodies, with a hole in the middle where the water drained off. The coffin was draped with a black velvet cloth with a large embroidered Star of David which was losing its silver threads. How narrow the coffin seemed, like a carton. Hard to believe there was enough room for Ludwig's body inside. Near the washing table was a bench on which lay Father's rolled-up pajamas, the blue-and-white striped ones that always made him look like a camp inmate. And next to the pajamas, a very large diaper the washers had forgotten to throw away.

8

In the course of the last hour, the mass of cars had moved forward a little. Mother and son had reached a spot over Father's thighs. Above them rose the huge superstructure of steel struts; standing beneath it felt like being in a cage for a dinosaur.

"You know what this sight reminds me of, very strongly?" Mother's throat was dry from heat, thirst, and shock. "It's like the golem still lying to this day in that synagogue attic. Wasn't it you who once told me the story?"

"Yes, but with the difference that the golem is made of clay, while what we are seeing here looks like flesh and blood. And the golem figure was much, much smaller than what's lying there under the bridge . . ."

"Don't say 'what's lying there' . . . say 'Papa.'"

"The golem was much smaller than . . . Papa."

According to legend, the "raging reporter" Egon Erwin Kisch, already famous by the time Father met him as a schoolboy, was supposed to have seen with his own eyes the golem's lifeless body in Prague. He had violated Rabbi Löw's strict prohibition of 1601 that no mortal must ever go up to the attic of the Old New Synagogue, the oldest in Europe, to look for the golem. When Ludwig asked him, "Is it true what they say about you, Egon Erwin? You really did see him, even though you wrote in your piece 'Looking for the Golem' that you had found nothing but dust and emptiness up there?" the famous Kisch didn't answer. But he did blush, from which Father concluded that the incident must have taken a different course, "because otherwise why would someone like Kisch turn red?!"

Ludwig's feet and legs lay to the right of Gustav and Mother, pointing west. His right leg, slightly bent, blocked their view of his crotch from where they were standing right now. Gustav got his pocket camera—the only one he owned—out of his luggage. Ludwig had been a passionate photographer. He owned ancient Nikons and a vintage Leica from 1935, which caused Gustav to generally refrain from taking pictures. But he always had his simple Kodak Instamatic along. He leaned far out over the railing. "Watch out!" Mother cried. "Have you lost your mind? You'll fall over the edge!" He photographed Ludwig's body as well as he could, saving the last two exposures for later.

Father lay on his left side—the heart side—the side he slept on in every bed in the world, ideally facing away from the windows, which absolutely had to be covered with black cloth. Even in hotel rooms in the most remote regions of the world, he had the windows covered with cloth if they didn't already have shutters. The room had to be absolutely dark. Father's ideal was not a single "lightcrack" anywhere. The room had to be dark as a tomb; he couldn't stand even a hair's breadth of light. It wasn't always easy to get hold of the right kind of cloth. He drove hotel porters to the brink of nervous breakdowns if their establishments lacked what he required. He needed thumbtacks as well to pin up the cloth, but they were easier to obtain than the material for blackout curtains. And despite all that, he also wore a sleeping mask even in the darkest rooms, and poopies pushed deep into his auditory canals— always and wherever he was.

His parents' sleep was sacrosanct and not to be disturbed. Their bedroom at home, however, was right next to Gustav's. It was inconceivable that they would ever have gotten up when he did. They slept until ten, by which time Gustav had already attended the first two periods of school. His nanny—always a different nanny, since none of them lasted more than two or three months under Mother's command, after which they either quit or were fired—his nanny of the moment had instructions to take a flashlight at seven a.m., creep up to the door of Gustav's room, which was left slightly ajar, and shine the beam at the boy's bed, jiggling it back and forth until he woke up. (Many failed to master the art of waking up the child and were fired on the spot.) The awakened Gustav thereupon waved in the direction of the cracked-open door as a sign he was awake and then had to tiptoe—and there had better not be a single creak from the parquet floor!—from his room into the corridor, and slink into the front part of the apartment where the bathroom was. His clothes had been prepared for him the day before and breakfast was waiting in the living room. Woe to him if he had forgotten something—a pencil, a compass, a book, a notebook! A return to his room was the equivalent of an Indian raid on a village of settlers, past the door of his parents' bedroom and then all the way back to the front door, where the nanny of the moment was waiting to bring him to his nearby school. Until he was thirteen and a half, the nanny accompanied him on the ten-minute walk so that no accident would befall him as he crossed two intersections.

"It's so unpleasant, very embarrassing indeed, to think that people could see Father like that," Mother whispered, pointing to Father's nakedness. "We've got to go farther up ahead, get right over his you-know-what, and then we'll throw a jacket or something else from your suitcase down onto him from the bridge." She never said the words penis or prick or cock. What euphemism had she used for it when he was a child? Gustav couldn't remember. He often heard her use the Viennese dialect word for prudish—"I'm *g'schamig*"— although it didn't accord with the facts: she wasn't particularly *g'schamig* at all. What was that word she used when he was a child—your thingee? your weenie? your jimmy? your johnson? your dong?

"Mother, what did you used to call my you-know-what? I can't remember."

"I can't remember either. This really isn't the time to be asking me that!"

What did Father call the male member—his own as well as his son's? Or did they never mention it by name?

Ludwig told Gustav the facts of life when he was ten. As so often, they were lying on the marital bed, father and son, in late afternoon twilight, while Ludwig yawned himself out. That's what he called the method he had invented to reenergize and refresh himself. He opened his mouth as wide as humanly possible and very quickly performed ten to fifteen mock yawns one right after the other. He did it so vigorously and so often that suddenly he would really begin to yawn, two dozen times in succession, and tears would flow from the corners of his eyes. Come, he would say, I'll yawn myself out and you lie down next to me and then I'll tell you something. Gustav listened attentively, and learned that the same organ a man used to make water also spilled the seed to sire children—so when you made water, the seed fell into the toilet bowl. That's how Gustav understood Father's explanation. And since he was much too embarrassed to ask for more details, he didn't pursue the matter any further. So, the man deposited his seed in the woman, where it united with an egg. And nine months later, that produced a boy or a girl. Gustav understood everything very well, although the procedure didn't seem very pleasant to him. So, from time to time, you spilled some seed —presumably while making water. Then you carefully retrieved it from the toilet bowl and put it into the woman's organ for making water. Whereupon a human being started grow-ing inside the woman. On the morning after his enlightenment, in the school bus that took him from the corner of Salesia-nergasse to the American School in the Bauernfeldgasse, Gustav explained what he had learned the previous day to a girl two years older than he. The girl was beside herself with excite-ment, surprise, and gratitude. At last she, too, finally knew where children came from. A pimply sixteen-year-old sitting behind them and listening closely to their conversation threat-ened to report Gustav to the principal's office for corrupting young girls on the school bus with obscene adult information. For weeks Gustav lived in fear that his tutorial would become known at school. From now on, teachers and fellow students of all ages would treat him with contempt and derision. But nothing happened at all.

Right up until Ludwig was seventy and his son in his mid-thirties, Father and son maintained their tradition of lying next to each other on the marital bed and talking. They called their horizontal conferences NLNRs: "no lights, no reading." It was a rare occasion for Father to interrupt his work for ten minutes —an event comparable to their urban circuits. The darkness, the twilight in the room, helped Father give himself a mar-velously thorough yawning-out. After ten or at most fifteen minutes of NLNR, he would plunge back into the heaps of unanswered mail, piles of newspapers and magazines, books and collected essays, that had accumulated during a week's absence giving lectures. On six days of the week, his mail consisted of pounds and pounds of bundles, neatly tied with twine and left on top of their mailbox by the postman. Among them several envelopes with unglued flaps bulged open, their contents spilling out: stacks of articles bulk-mailed at a discount by *Argus*, the Berlin clipping service that Father had engaged to comb through every German-language newspaper, no matter how tiny its circulation, and look for mention of his name. And so pounds of articles clipped from regional and national newspapers were delivered to their house every month at the rate for printed matter. They mentioned Ludwig Rubin at more or less length, yet often only in passing, as one among many at a convention, demonstration, or in a delegation. Some clippings reported on one of his discoveries or theories while others praised or condemned one of his lectures or publications. Not infrequently, reports from German, Austrian, and Swiss wire services were reprinted a hundred times, by every regional paper, the same three or four lines over and over again. For example: "During the symposium 'Man and the Environment' in Giessen, the American scientist Ludwig Rubin suggested that the pharmaceutical company Bayer develop a pair of 'virus glasses.' According to Rubin, one could detect and successfully avoid pathogens in the future with the help of such an invention."

If Father was on the road for more than three or four days, the manifold mailings would grow into hills. After a week or so, Gustav would cut open the bundles and begin to sort letters from printed matter, books from newspapers, magazines from advertisements. He arranged the newspapers and magazines into piles until his constructions resembled the cords of firewood one sees stacked along the walls of Alpine farmhouses. And so during Father's travels, a huge orderly heap gradually accumulated. Hardly had Ludwig returned than he began to destroy it, picking it apart and gradually disassembling it, until everything ended up in tall garbage bags, together with the mountains of clippings sent by the Argus company, named after the hundred-eyed giant of antiquity. And then Father took off on another trip and the towers of mail began to rise anew.

"Are you coming or not, Burschi? We've really got to do something, right away!"

They returned to the Cadillac, opened the trunk, and Gustav pawed through the big red suitcase, which was seriously overstuffed and much too heavy—he had brought an absurd number of presents for the children. He showed Mother a brown wool jacket he didn't like very much; Madeleine had given it to him.

"That's good, that's good. It's so hideous; where did you get it? Em must have given it to you, right? Put on an undershirt now. It's sure to start getting cool."

He handed Rosa the wool jacket and locked the trunk without putting on an undershirt. They worked their way over to the edge of the bridge, this time aiming for a spot a good deal farther east. Gustav felt increasingly certain that the hallucination would not be repeated. The colossal, golemlike fatherbody would have disappeared.

He looked down at the river.

Father lay there unchanged.

Gustav closed his eyes and opened them again as wide as he could. He watched Rosa spread out the wool jacket on a steel beam flecked with rust spots, and then throw it down into the abyss with both hands. The wind blew the piece of clothing away under the bridge, toward the north side, where it quickly disappeared beneath the waves. It had not occurred to either of them that even had the jacket landed on its target, it would have covered only a tiny piece of his nakedness. For more they would have needed an oversized bedspread—but where could they conjure one up here?

"Give me the phone. I have to call Bee this minute and tell her what's happening to us." Babette, whom Mother called Bee, was Rosa's best and only friend. She was just a few years older than Gustav, a photographer from Vienna who had moved to New York hoping to find more and better work than in her native Austria. But she found no work, and Mother supported her financially. Bee often stayed with her in the untidy apartment on Central Park until she started a new relationship. Bee liked influential, well-to-do, imperious women. She would move into the house, hotel room, or apartment of a new partner until, after a few days or weeks—seldom as long as several months—the love affair came to an end, and then she would return to Mother until she stumbled into her next passion. She helped out with the housework, for there was nothing Mother hated more than running a house—cooking, dishwashing, vacuuming, bed making, laundering. Babette took care of all that for as long as she stayed with Mother. No sooner had she left than the apartment sank back into its Sleeping Beauty paralysis again. No one listened to Mother as attentively as Babette. No one loved and revered Mother so unreservedly as Babette. If she found a tissue with the imprint of Rosa's lips in

the bathroom just after Mother had applied or removed lipstick and then dabbed her mouth and thrown the Kleenex into
the toilet bowl, Babette would not relieve herself there under
any circumstances. It was inconceivable for her to desecrate
and then simply flush away that gauzy paper floating there in
the water with the perfect image of Mother's lips.

"It's me. Listen to this, Bee, you're not going to believe
a word of it . . ." She began with Gustav's late arrival and his
blunder at the car rental, then retraced every exhausting moment of the trip they had suffered through so far, right up to
the point when they had first caught sight of Father under the
bridge.

While Mother talked on the telephone, Gustav dozed off. He
awoke feeling much more tired and run down than he had
before his little siesta. Mother handed the phone back to him.
"Bee doesn't believe a word of it!" He noticed immediately
that the battery of the little apparatus was completely used up.
Quite apart from the huge per-minute cost, there wasn't an
ounce of charge left on the cell phone; Rosa had talked to her
friend for more than half an hour.

"She really made me laugh, Bee did. There's no one else
I laugh that much with . . ."

"What was so funny?" He stretched his arms in all directions. Every muscle hurt. He was feeling more jet-lagged than
he ever had in his life.

"What was so funny? She says what we're seeing down
there is a 'father morgana' . . ." Rosa was still laughing. "Don't
you think that's funny?"

Madeleine wouldn't be able to reach them anymore, nor could they call the house on the lake. Gustav scolded, yelled at Mother the way he had as a child when she stayed on the phone too long. Then, if she didn't end her conversation, he would bang the doors and slam the milk-glass door of his room shut behind him. During one of these temper tantrums, the insert, as tall as a grown-up, shattered. A thousand shards of glass lay mingled with the hundreds of Lego bricks spread out on the floor. It took days for him to separate the Legos from the splinters. Years later, in the gray-brown Lego sack smelling of wax, plastic, and stale air, he would still find fragments of glass now and then, cut himself on them, and bleed. Every time he cut his finger after that, he would think of Mother's excessive use of the telephone—orgies of calls which, in later years after he had left home, involved him more than anyone else. Even back before there were cell phones, Rosa would pursue him with telephone calls, every day, every night, no matter where he might be. Every time a telephone rang, no matter where, he knew it was she. By devious means, crooked paths, and chains of calls she would have managed to find out where he was at the moment, whether in a ski cabin near Pontresina, on a café terrace in Rome, with friends in their Paris penthouse, or in a hotel in London, Dublin, or New York. She always found out where he was. And called him up. As soon as a telephone rang in his vicinity, he would predict: It's my mom! Nobody believed him. But he was right.

"You shouldn't have let me call Bee. You know me better than that. You know what I'm like. When your father was starting to run after me, we used to talk on the phone a great deal. I was already in Vienna; he was still in New York. He was so cute. He told me, 'Other men spoil their women with fur coats. I'm going to treat you to long-distance calls.'"

"I already know the story, Mom. You really are the queen of excuses."

"And don't forget, transatlantic calls were extremely expensive in those days! Three or four dollars a minute!"

"I know, Mama. You've both told me all about it."

"OK. I'm thirsty now. Go get us something to drink. And I'm hungry, too. Those few raisins certainly weren't enough."

He had already noticed that Joe's Dog House, the mobile takeout stand some distance away from them, had opened its fold-down counters and begun to sell its inventory. The vehicle's generator was droning so loudly it could have been producing current for a small city. Gustav had hoped to avoid having to wait in the long line and so hadn't mentioned the possibility of getting a little something to eat and drink. But now he had no choice, he had to stand in line. But when he arrived at the run-down vehicle whose long side was adorned with the yellowed image of a hush puppy, Gustav discovered that Joe and his brother Jack had already sold out all their food and drink half an hour ago. Not a package of popcorn or a chocolate bar, not even a drop of liquid or a piece of bread to be had. In a flash the stand's owners had been inundated with money, even though they had charged three, four—at the end even ten times their usual price.

On his way back to his mother, Gustav bought a bottle of ice-cold mineral water from a Mexican who had suddenly materialized out of thin air on the bridge; he paid $7.50 for a twelve-ounce bottle.

Rosa drank in eager gulps. She left two fingers of water for her son, handing him the bottle with the words, "Sorry, Schatzi, I was so thirsty!"

We're different. We're different from the others, Gustav. That's what Father had taught his son. We have no relatives. We outlived our parents and we're embarrassed about it. Your mother's parents were driven into cattle cars while we managed to escape, Rosa and I. We ran away from death: I to the safety of Switzerland, your mother via Spain and Portugal to America. And now we're ashamed to be alive. To take my mind off it, to distract myself every day, I started a family with your mother. Her experience was much the same as mine, and she had even fewer relatives to begin with. We're different from other parents, Mom and I.

Father, mother, child. The three of us, created from one flesh, we're Siamese triplets, attached at the head and the genitals. And behind us, the dead. Ludwig, Rosa, Gustav. Rosa, Gustav, Ludwig. Gustav, Ludwig, Rosa. No siblings. One aunt who had a falling-out with Mother after the war. A cousin, the daughter of that aunt, whom he'd never met. Two uncles who died young. No grandparents. Mother's parents were gassed. Father's mother escaped from an internment camp in Gurs, in the south of France, but died soon after the war was over. Father's father had succumbed to food poisoning before the war. What luck, Ludwig often repeated, that my father died from unpasteurized beer before the years of hell even began.

Gustav had grown up without relatives, without grandparents, aunts, uncles, cousins, nieces, nephews. I'm all alone, he cursed, so goddamn alone. My parents are all I have.

You and only you give meaning to our lives, Father drummed into his son. You are all your mother and I have. That's why there's nothing unusual about you coming to our hotel room and sitting on the foot of our bed to have break-fast with us, even though you're thirty, thirty-five years old. To this day, you sit there cross-legged at the foot of your par-ents' double bed when we're on a trip, and you have breakfast with us, just like you used to as a child. It's nice, right? It's the way things should be. Be happy we're still alive. Someday when we're not around anymore, you'll long to dig us up out of the ground again, just you wait and see. I'm sorry, but you'll just have to accept that we're more attached to you than normal parents are to their children. You haven't suffered too much from it, have you? After the war, all we had left was the feel-ing of belonging together as a family. You embody the feeling that binds our family together, Gustav. You are us. I am the two of you. Rosa is us. We are you. We are one flesh united, a unit of Rubinflesh.

And yet Gustav always had the impression that he didn't look Jewish at all. When he happened to be among Jewish men, women, and children, he was even embarrassed about his un-Jewish appearance. Seldom did Jews he met for the first time believe him when he said he was Jewish. Every time, he had to insist upon it, had to fight to be counted among them, struggle to win their unqualified trust. If people saw him with his parents, Gustav breathed a sigh of relief—Jewishness wasn't exactly written all over their faces, either, but people were more ready to accept their ancestry than Gustav's. Now they'll finally believe that I belong! But then it occurred to him, people still might think I'm a Gentile child they adopted.

In the fall of 1945, when Mother was thirty years old, she learned that her parents had almost certainly perished, and a broad strand of her hair turned white as snow overnight. She suddenly became unable to walk, spent months in bed. Karl Bühler, a pupil of Sigmund Freud's, whom Rosa sought out in New York as soon as she was able to take a hundred steps again without collapsing, advised her, "You've got to bring children into the world. That's the only way you're going to survive: as a mother, as the founder of a new family." Gustav, her only child, became Rosa's survival. "We are one flesh united, my parents and me," Gustav told his first girlfriends, and he also explained it to Madeleine, who had assumed that in time, she would be able to relax if not entirely dissolve his attachment to his parents.

Just when Gustav was sinking deeper and deeper into a debauched life that gave him little joy and much pain and shame, Richard Lichtmann had found this religious daughter of a family of French textile dealers for his friend. "In the Talmud," Lichtmann taught him, "it says it's more difficult for God to bring two people together who were meant for each other than it was to part the Red Sea, back when the Jews were fleeing Pharaoh's army. But I'm going to find the right woman for you. I already have someone in mind. She's the daughter of one of our most loyal customers, from way back when my father was running the business." Richard was trying to turn Gustav into an Orthodox Jew, and he would eventually succeed. It was hard to believe, but thanks to Madeleine, Licht-mann's friend gradually turned into a pious Jew. The anarchist began to observe Shabbat and follow the dietary laws. He no longer attended synagogue just on the High Holy Days. He took every letter of the Torah to heart—yet still remained the Mommy and Daddy's boy he had always been, the third of the unit of Rubinflesh. Mother was furious: "You're not just turn-ing pious, which already makes me completely nervous, you're living with a Sephardic woman to boot. They don't fit in with us. That should be obvious. At first I thought she had a lot of spirit, but it's just her asthma. Couldn't you at least have found yourself a healthy woman to marry? It had to be a semi-invalid? Where did we go wrong, your father and I, for you to lose your way and make such a bad choice?"

But the woman he lived with and thought he loved did not become the center of his life. No, the foundation of his existence remained Father and Mother. "Even when my par-ents have disappeared," he tried to explain to Madeleine, "I'll still be connected to them. I can already sense it. I'm afraid you'll have to prepare yourself mentally for that, my angel. Even in death, they will still be monitoring my missteps and con-demning my failures as they always did in their lifetime. All survivors listen to the voices of their dead until they themselves must die, leaving behind children who listen. And perhaps it's a good thing that we carry such wistfulness within us as long as we live and are forced to encounter our fathers and mothers in dreams and daydreams, over and over, our whole life long. It's vital to break free of one's parents, but it's quite impos-sible, if truth be told."

9

Mother and son stood high above Father's sex. Although at rest in death, it was still several yards long and lay stretched out west to east, lapped by the foaming current and surrounded by flotsam: plastic bottles, chunks of wood, seaweed, and branches. Then it freed itself again, came into clear, sharp view. It looked shriveled and as if petrified, white and gray and not very attractive. Gustav was disturbed by the foreskin that narrowed down to the tip. Even as a child, he'd been embarrassed by the fact that Father wasn't circumcised. His own circumcision had happened the day after he was born, in Elmhurst Hospital in Queens, not for religious reasons but because in the 1950s, all male babies born in America were circumcised unless their parents raised an objection before their birth. Ludwig flew into a rage when he learned of his son's medical circumcision, not because it had been done, but because he, the nonbeliever, had wanted the religious ceremony: the traditional circumcision eight days after the birth, carried out by a mohel, the ritual circumciser. He wanted his son, at least, to get what his assimilated parents denied him. He decided to sue the hospital and the surgeon who had performed the operation, and he engaged the help of a lawyer friend of his. He rounded up a group of friends and acquaintances and was going to have them march up and down in front of the main entrance holding picket signs saying Don't Give Birth At Elmhurst! or They Cut Without Asking! or Boys Beware! or Boys Boycott Elmhurst! By the fourth day after the birth, Rosa was able to calm her husband down enough to at least persuade him to abandon this plan. She convinced him that he would only make a fool of himself.

Thirty-five years later, the problem of circumcision cropped up for Gustav again. For months, several rabbis had been giving him instruction, helping him find the path to the heart of the Torah and complete his return to the fold, his *teshuvah*, as it was called. They urged him to listen to his conscience and his heart and get himself circumcised a second time before marrying Madeleine. But how can a foreskin that's no longer there be removed again? You have to let them stick a large silver needle into the edge of your glans until enough blood runs out, whereupon a rabbi speaks a blessing and bestows a Hebrew name upon the double-circumcisee. Only then does a male Jew who for whatever reason has not been circumcised strictly, according to ritual, become a full-fledged member of the denomination. If he chooses not to undergo this ceremony, however, he is regarded as a *mamzer*, a sort of bastard. Gustav kept putting off the event, no matter how much Madeleine pleaded with him to finally get it done right.

Amadée, however, had the good fortune to receive a proper circumcision, eight days after his birth, in a shul in the Grünangergasse in Vienna. Gustav looked away as the mohel made the brisk excision and then put the tip of the screaming newborn's bloody cock into his mouth for a few seconds. For that's what all the circumcisers do, at every circumcision. They fill their mouth with red wine and then they kiss the freshly circumcised penis in order to disinfect it and dull the pain. Amadée was given the Hebrew name Aharon ben Reuben, son of Reuben, because Reuben was the Hebrew name the rabbis gave Gustav even though he didn't let them stick him in the glans.

"We've really got to do something. It can't go on like this, Gustav. You've got to see what you can do," Rosa begged. "Please do something. We can't just leave him lying there like that. You can see his butt cheeks, too!"

"What do you want me to do, Mom? I can't get into the river and swim to him. And besides, what would I do then?"

"Where there's a will, there's a way. One time in Hollywood, when I was young, there was a party at Errol Flynn's house and I kneeled right down in front of Ernst Lubitsch, because I worshiped him, of course. I was in awe of him. He put his gigantic hand on my head and said, 'Remember one thing, *Kinderl*, something to cherish your whole life long: you can achieve anything with willpower. Anything.'"

"But it won't work to throw something down onto him from here, Mom. You tried it already. Nobody's aim is that good, whether you're throwing clothes or blankets or whatever. And besides, nobody knows it's our Papa lying down there!"

"We're only imagining this whole thing, anyway. I'm going to ask a few people what they see. You come, too. Then we'll decide what to do."

She approached a tanned youth who was sunning himself at the bridge railing. "Excuse me, mister," she began, and explained that she had lost her purse. Maybe it had fallen over the railing. Could he take a look down there? Maybe he could see something. He squinted at her. If her purse had gone over the railing, she would have had to throw it. And that couldn't have happened, could it? No, he had no intention of looking down. He didn't even say sorry.

An older woman was sitting in the opened door of her Saab, peeling an orange, and Mother asked if she could take a moment of her time; she had a favor to ask. The woman finished peeling the fruit, divided it in two, laid the peeled halves on the dashboard, and got out of her car.

"You have marvelous blue eyes," the woman said. "They're so bright and clear. I've seldom seen such fascinating eyes. They're more beautiful and intense than your son's . . . assuming this gentleman is your son."

Mother thanked the stranger for the compliment and winked proudly at Gustav.

After looking down from the bridge for a minute, the woman said, "It's very odd. I feel like there's a . . . gigantic, naked body of a man lying down there. But the weirdest thing is that those rock formations look like my husband, Captain Selfridges of the United States Navy. He died eight years ago."

"Rock formations?" asked Rosa.

"Yes, rock formations. What else could they be?" answered the old lady. She gave Rosa a curious look.

"You're right," Mother replied, "what else could they be?"

Mother was going to approach a little girl next. She was playing Trivial Pursuit with her older brother in the bed of a pickup truck. At the last moment, Gustav held Mother back from involving children in something that was sure to be extremely confusing to them.

A man with a receding hairline and a friendly grin walked up to them. He was wearing a red silk shirt sprinkled with yellow stars, tucked into earth-colored brown shorts. "Gene Wesley Elder's the name. Pleased to meet you. Have you filmed me yet? No? Don't you have a video camera?"

Rosa looked at him with such a combination of exhaustion and hostility that if nature had conferred upon Mr. Elder even the slightest bit of sensitivity, he would have taken to his heels immediately.

"All the same, Mother, perhaps we could ask him—"

"Ask me—ask me anything. Your wish is my command. You see, I'm an artist, from San Antonio, site of the famous Battle of the Alamo. Reality is my movie screen, if you dig what I mean. I've been in thousands of amateur films. Wherever there's tourists, I push my way into their videos. You can see me all over the world, back home, when your trips are over! People are surprised to see me. Who's that? they wonder. Who's that guy waving, with the silly grin? Well, it's me, it's Gene Wesley Elder! You're amazed, madame. I can see it by the look in your eye. How can a guy who's almost fifty years old pull such a stunt? But it's not a stunt. It's art. A traffic jam like this is the perfect hunting ground for me. Take a guess: how many people would you say have taken a picture of me in the last few hours, whether they knew it or not?"

"Please," Rosa interrupted the cheery man with a small silver stud glittering in his left earlobe, "have the goodness to understand that I've been through a really difficult day. I need some peace and quiet."

"Peace and quiet? As a prisoner of fate on the Tappan Zee Bridge? As Manitou's hostage? Do you realize it's the god of the Indians who's keeping us here? Right here, today, he's sole ruler over this area. We find ourselves in the heart of ancient Indian lands." Mr. Elder scratched his left thigh, covered with coarse, black hair. "Come on, take it easy! Have a little fun. It'll do you good. Anyways, as I said before, I turn up in people's home videos all over the world. To think of all the places I've been videoed in! I merge art and life, transform clueless tourists into art collectors, no matter where they're from: Ada, Oklahoma, or Campbell, Idaho; Akron, Ohio, or Butterfield, California!"

"Thank you so much for your remarks," Mother replied. "Would you now permit us to be on our way without pestering us any further? It's been months since I've seen my son and I'd like to be alone with him, thank you very much."

"I only wanted to provide a bit of pleasure, madame, that's all. Have a nice day! And don't forget, everything in nature has the form of a sphere, a cone, or a cylinder."

He strolled off toward a guy with long Rasta braids hanging down his back.

"Hi, I'm Gene Wesley Elder. Do you want to film me?"

"I've never met such a pain in the neck, and I've known a lot of pains in the neck in my time," Rosa Rubin growled. "And did you notice that stupid *Flinserl* in his ear? Men who wear a small earring hope for nothing more than to be asked about just that: why they're wearing it, who gave them the idea, where they got it from, and so on and so forth. You can really unnerve them by ignoring their *Flinserl*, pretending not to see it. It drives them half crazy!"

They turned to a man and woman trying to go for a stroll between the cars: "May I ask you a favor?" She explained to the couple that her purse had fallen off the bridge. The pair looked over the railing and saw the water, the bridge pier, flecks of froth, and, in fact, a small black purse lying down there. For sure, yes, quite sure, it was small and black.

"My God, what idiots!" Mother declared as they moved on, and from then on, she asked no one else for help.

Gustav looked down at the river. There it lay, his father's body, over a mile long, majestic, stark naked.

Until Gustav was fourteen or fifteen, his parents would take baths with him, in the same bathtub. Until he was seventeen—or even longer, until he left home—they would walk around the apartment with no clothes on. Lying in the bathtub, Father often gave his son advice about how to lead his life. With his kneecaps protruding from the water and his body dimly visible beneath the islands of foam, Ludwig proposed life strategies and helped the growing boy make decisions. His son sat on the toilet lid and listened to his father. He regarded Ludwig as his mentor and teacher. In comparison to what Ludwig taught him, the schools he attended were headquarters of wasted time. Not until he was twenty did he start to find his father's advice less and less valuable—a mistake he began to regret at age forty.

Until he was sixteen, he loved slipping into the marital bed on Sunday morning or late in the forenoon (on Sundays, his parents stayed extra long in bed). He lay between them, he in his pajamas and Father and Mother naked. Gustav was a bridge, embedded between his parents. They leaned across him to kiss each other and covered him with kisses as well. Sometimes, in the midst of being kissed, he dived down and disappeared beneath the immense featherbed, crept "underground" into imagined living spaces, nurseries, closets.

During forty-eight years of marriage, Father always lay on the left side of the bed, Mother on the right. There were no exceptions, not even for one night. Mother could only sleep on the right, Father on the left. And when they walked together side by side, on errands in town or on hikes or on the stairway of the State Opera, Ludwig was always on Rosa's left, never on her right.

Decades later, Gustav could still feel the kisses Mother would give him on the tip of his tongue as he lay in the middle of their bed. Even as a fourteen-year-old, he would encircle the tip of Rosa's tongue with his own. Father would then pretend to be jealous. Is it really necessary to amuse yourself in bed with other men when you've got me? Years later, when Gustav asked her about these scenes, Rosa replied, "You're making that up. What nonsense. You're just trying to make yourself interesting and me look like an impossible person. You tell other people fairy tales about me. Or perhaps you wish it had been that way. But I never gave you tongue kisses, ever. I'm absolutely certain of that. Such rubbish . . ."

Mother's bush and Father's uncircumcised penis, his curly pubic hair, tinged with gray and white, were an integral part of Gustav's childhood and youth. He was sixteen, however, before he understood where a man penetrated a woman. Below the belly? he thought, where little girls have their slit? It wasn't finally revealed to him that the gate to paradise was hidden between the legs until the first of Father's glossy magazines fell into his hands. Ludwig brought them home from his trips and buried them in diverse yellow, red, and blue plastic bags. These skin mags were hidden deep within packs of daily newspapers, clippings, illustrated Sunday supplements, or in the middle of a pile of essays and abstracts Father had brought home from a convention or a conference. In full color: splayed-out legs, moist tongues, parted lips, and all of it covered with ejaculate. Gustav came upon more and more thick, glossy, full-color magazines in Ludwig's plastic bags. And the more he found, the more he wanted to see. His sweet addiction drove him to look in all the hiding places in all the attics and all the cellars. Everywhere Father stored paper, naked, copulating women were embedded among the books, magazines, and newspapers.

On the eighth floor of an ugly modern building on the Danube Canal in Vienna, Ludwig had a small apartment he used to work in. One room was used to store the books, unopened newspapers and magazines, and tons of old paper he would never sort through again but still couldn't bear to part with. He called the room his mine, but Gustav called it Paper Hell. Whoever entered it was confronted by mountains of printed matter that reached to the shoulder of an adult and up to the forehead of a child. At the other end of the room, a small streak of light was visible. The rest of the window was blocked by the mass of paper. If you wanted to move around in there, you had to clamber up onto the piles and then cross the universe of information as if aboard a giant raft, adrift on the high seas. Here and there you would sink in up to your calves, then scale new heights, and eventually reach the far wall, where the narrow slice of window looked down onto the city, the second district, the gray Danube Canal, the giant Ferris wheel. En route, Gustav would kneel down, plunge his hands into the depths, and pull one or another of the plastic bags up to the surface as if weighing anchor. Then he would paw through the smooth, bulging bag as though it were a treasure chest and find more magazines with brand-new, never-before-seen images of ejaculation. They were all alike, yet his desire for more and more magazines kept surging up. They stoked his appetite, goaded him to keep looking, keep digging until he was completely exhausted. He thought of his precious discoveries as nuggets. Every time he crossed Paper Hell it was like looking for gold in the Yukon, and when he held a new nugget in his hand, he was suffused with the voluptuous pleasure of a successful gold miner. In the first decade of his sexual maturity, his desire for nuggets exceeded his desire for real flesh and blood, women's kisses, women's warmth, lovemaking.

And Father? What did he do with this avalanche of magazines?

"When I was a boy, and later, when I was a young man," Father confided to his son, "I would never lock the door of the men's room on a train or in a restaurant, in hopes that someone would open the door and see me standing there with my exposed dick in my hand. Did you ever do that?"

"No, Father, never. It wouldn't even occur to me . . ."

"Strange . . . how different we are!"

There were certain tapes Ludwig saved. Gustav tracked them down, too, in the depths of the plastic bags: the documents of Father's amorous adventures in foreign cities, in distant lands, recorded in hotels or the apartments of his innumerable conquests. While riding toward climax, he would often have a small cassette recorder running. Ludwig's son was capable only of listening to these recordings for a few minutes at a time, although he planned eventually to play them one after another, all the way through. The tapes were preserved in ordinary business envelopes and labeled with words like "Throw away!," "Defective!" "Blank!" or "Unimportant!" They were the evidence of Ludwig's adulteries, beginning a few days after his marriage and ending just prior to his stroke, an obsession which Gustav envied his father. More than any other force in his life,

it was this drive, this preoccupation that defined and constituted Ludwig. The chase after the moisture of young women,
the flesh of breasts, the lips of ladies drove him into a fury. It
was his only true passion and outstripped by far all the effort
he ever put into his career, all his professional ambition. His
lust to sleep with women—with young women if at all possible, for money if necessary—was the true elixir of his life.
"I feel it's the greatest miracle on this earth whenever I see a
beautiful woman," he said. "Compared to such a miracle, the
miracle of a woman's body, I couldn't care less about all the
rockets and supersonic jets, all the nuclear research my colleagues or I have ever done, all our technical and scientific
accomplishments. Just the way a woman trembles when you
kiss her! Every woman I pass, whether it's in Paris, London,
New York, or Vienna, in Rome, Madrid, or Tokyo, I imagine myself making *furious* love to her. I put together mental
lists of the women I've sighted and who may have the potential to become my mistresses. There's only one condition:
they have to be younger than forty. So here's how the game
goes: I take a close look at a woman strolling past me. No, I
think, not that one, nor the next, nor the third, nor the fourth.
But the fifth one—perfect! So the score is one in five, three
in ten, five in twenty, and so on until a hundred women and
girls have passed me. Believe me, there's never more than
twenty women in a hundred—twenty-two at the most—who
have the potential. Although I did reach the highest quota
ever on an April day in the year 1967, in Paris, more pre-
cisely in the sixth and seventh arrondissements: thirty-one in
a hundred!"

Gustav longed to be able to keep pace with Ludwig's amazing vitality. The list of his own conquests by the time he got married constituted only a fraction of his father's, and it hadn't gotten much longer since the wedding. On the contrary, he had little desire or ability to add anything worth mentioning to his total.

On principle and without exception, Ludwig Rubin referred to the act of love as a "number." "My God," he gasped on one of the tapes, recorded at a time when he was a good deal older than sixty, "was that ever an amazing number. Our best yet!" "Yes! I was just about to say the same thing. It was great," agreed a woman's indistinct voice. "It still is," Father insisted, for he hadn't withdrawn yet. "Now I know why I was born: for moments like this." And a few minutes later, he was hanging over the edge of the bed with a flushed face, his mouth close to the microphone on the floor beneath it, whispering so his lover wouldn't hear, "My God, was that a good number! Wonderful! A marvelous number, a marvelous number, a wonderful number! I hope I got it all on tape!"

"My only consolation," said Mother, again looking down at Father's gigantic penis and colossal butt cheeks, "is that I know for certain he was always faithful to me, with one or two tiny exceptions. He was with one woman—I think it was in Cannes or Nice—in a museum. I found two tickets in his pocket and asked him, why two tickets, Ludwig? He began stuttering and then confessed that he'd been to the museum with 'someone.' And then that idiotic woman who wrote that she needed him to send her money to pay for an abortion. And he was stupid enough to leave the letter lying where I was sure to find it. We fought for days. We had to send you out on walks with your nanny all the time. Maybe you remember. But those were the only exceptions, thank God."

The summer Gustav spent in Juan-les-Pins with his parents and his nanny Erna Schuster was particularly hot. They had rented a vacation apartment in an ugly Côte-d'Azur highrise. He could still hear the loud crunch of the large, dry, brown leaves underfoot in the courtyard of the building, which he and Erna had to circle again and again until his parents were done fighting. Years later, Ludwig told his son who had written the letter demanding money. "For years she was my main lover. One day she gave me an ultimatum: either you leave your family or I'm moving to Brazil!" From then on, father and son always referred to her as "the Brazilian."

In my next life, Father often said, I'm going to marry a Japanese woman. Why Japanese? Gustav would ask. A Japanese woman waits on her husband, Ludwig replied, and doesn't ask any unpleasant questions. She takes off his street shoes and puts on his slippers. She runs him a hot bath. She cooks for him, puts the food on the table, and pours his sake. Whenever he wants a lover, she's at his disposal in bed. One can't say that your mother possesses many attributes of a Japanese woman. But in my next life . . .

On this Tappan Zee afternoon, Gustav made no attempt to shake the foundations of Rosa's belief in Father's faithfulness. He'd tried to disabuse her of it earlier, without the least success. She had trust in Father's moral strength. That he snuggled up to her at night was proof enough for her of his boundless affection—even of his desire and capacity to love her. Even after their big scenes, no matter how much they had fought, they cuddled up tight with each other at night. And everything was all right again. Or almost all right.

"When I see him lying there like that, I remember how we'd be snuggled up and ready to go to sleep and he'd always have to tell me about Canada so I could fall asleep . . . I couldn't do it without hearing about Canada." In the late Forties, Ludwig had taken a trip across Canada. He'd gone from Montreal to Vancouver to attend one of the first conferences on nuclear fusion. He traveled by train, since back then he was still observing Rosa's strict rule against flying. For days, mountains, lakes, forests, and prairies rolled past the windows, one landscape resembling the other almost completely. In just a few minutes, Father's depiction and description of Canada could put Mother into a deep sleep.

"And you? Were you just as virtuous as Father?" Gustav asked.

"What do you mean?"

"Were you just as faithful to him as he was to you?"

"That's not something you ask your mother."

"I'm asking you anyway."

"Just use your imagination. You have that much imagination, don't you? Besides, I intrigued him up to the end, I really did. I mean he was interested in me physically, too. I just told you that earlier today, didn't I? Is your memory that short? How sad: my only child has the memory of a lizard."

10

Bawling children, loud laughter, music from a hundred car radios, male and female voices of countless newscasters, arguments between people exhausted from the wait—the noise on the bridge was reaching an almost unbearable level. Soda and ice cream vendors popped up out of nowhere, a whole troop of sixteen- and seventeen-year-old Mexican boys this time. They walked along the bridge, laughing, waving their ice-cold wares. Within minutes they were sold out, disappeared, soon to return with more. A hostile crowd encircled the snow-white stretch limo now. "Open up!" they shouted. "You've got booze in there, in your cool little bar, and we've got nothing. Give us some! Who's in there, anyway?" Rumors had been circulating since the beginning: Leonardo DiCaprio was in there. Somebody had recognized him when he opened the window for a few seconds. No, it was Tom Cruise and Penélope Cruz in the back, no doubt about it. Nonsense, replied others, the cardinal of Baltimore was sitting in there. Somebody else said the car belonged to Violet String, Mayor Giuliani's favorite prostitute, everybody knew that. The one-way-mirror windows remained closed. There was no sign of life, however impatient the shouting became.

A big helicopter flew low over the waiting crowd. The clatter of the rotor was so loud people ducked their heads. They could see the red cross on the copter's belly. Seconds later, it landed on the east bank of the Hudson. In the immediate vicinity of the bridgehead there was a small landing pad for just such emergencies.

The reason for the rescue operation spread like wildfire: a motorist had suffered a heart attack. Pushing a stretcher on wheels, four medics ran down the bumpy, traffic-free side of the bridge where the construction was going on, moving in the opposite direction from the traffic jam. They passed close by Gustav and his mother. Rosa tried to call out to them, but they ignored her.

"Not very friendly, that emergency crew," she remarked. "I just wanted to ask them what happened."

Ten minutes later they returned with a patient on the stretcher. The owner of the trailer, the former stationmaster of Victoria Station, lay there with an oxygen mask pressed to his face and his eyes shut tight. His face was so furrowed and battered, it resembled ancient architecture. There was something parchmentlike about his wrinkles. His glasses with the crack in them were askew, having slid down next to his temple.

There goes one more piece of my childhood, carried away with that old man, Gustav felt. My sleeping car trips from Vienna to London, crossing the channel in gently rocking ships. When I woke up in the night, the thirty-car train was still on the rails, but the rails were in the dark belly of a steamship. My bed was gently rocking, the sleeping car creaking.

"I shouldn't say anything," Rosa said, "but I have very little sympathy for that man. Anybody who's such a nasty person, it's going to affect their heart sooner or later. The way he looked at me! If he looked into the water, he'd kill all the fish!"

He had begun to put his toilet at the disposal of drivers in need for a fee of ten dollars per person. He had already taken in about three hundred dollars when he suffered the heart attack. People said that he had collapsed excitedly uttering the words "God bless America!" In the distance, Gustav could see that in the meantime a huge crowd of people had gathered around the trailer, not an organized group waiting their turn patiently, but an image of anarchy.

When Ludwig was almost fifty, Gustav started fearing that in the long run, his father would not be up to the stress of his schedule of constant worldwide traveling, lecturing, and panel discussions and would have an infarct. No sooner was he back from one international commitment than he was getting ready for the next. Did he overwork himself on purpose, systematically, hoping to be struck down some day, to drop dead in the midst of activity? Unpack, pack. Empty the suitcases, fill the suitcases.

When he still traveled by sleeping car, Gustav and Rosa would accompany him to the Westbahnhof in Vienna every time he left. Once, on his way to Copenhagen and leaning out of the train window as usual to say good-bye, he suddenly clutched at his chest. "Burschi, what's wrong?" Mother was very alarmed. He turned chalk-white, left the window, and jumped back down onto the platform. "For heaven's sake, what's wrong with you?" asked Rosa. He had left his passport at home. "Who am I?" he cried, and repeated, "Who am I?!" The trip to Denmark was postponed for twenty-four hours.

"One of the main reasons I'm always on the go is your mother, of course," Father explained upon returning from his trips. "I just can't take her. After a few days, I'm so exhausted! I've got to recuperate. Although . . . if I'm gone for more than two days, she already comes to join me. I would turn down many lecture invitations, but I accept them just to escape Mother for a moment and not have her continually by my side. And yet I love her, believe me, I really do. Then I come back home and cling to her at night: that's how it has to be. And by the next day, unfortunately, she's really getting on my nerves again."

Gustav was afraid that Father would die before Mother did. She wouldn't be able to exist without Ludwig, he thought —without support, without anchor, looking back on a life that must seem unfulfilled to her, without parents, without siblings, with nothing but an adult son whose most fervent wish was to escape the circle of her power and influence.

"So, let me tell you what's been going on with me since our last walk together. Basically, it was a rather typical week of traveling for me, as you'll see." That's how Father opened the conversation as they began a new circuit just a few days before his seventieth birthday. They were walking through Vienna, along narrow, cobblestone streets, across bridges, over park lawns, across squares. They traversed the Kahlenberg. And as Ludwig began talking, he inserted the formulaic phrase that mother, father, and son used every time they were reunited after an absence: "since last we parted."

"Now then, since last we parted . . . On November third I took the train from Vienna to Munich and then from Munich to Berlin. I arrived in Berlin on the last train of the day, went to the Hotel Schweizerhof, and worked until one in the morning on my lecture for the Lions Club the next day. That's something like the Rotary Club—overweight businessmen with presumably good intentions. They get together like the Masons and make big speeches. As usual, I didn't have anything prepared. I was dead tired and went to bed shortly after one. I had the desk wake me at six-thirty and wrote down key words until nine, when the car came for me. Some guy picked me up and drove me to the Kongresshalle—you know, that huge building the Berliners call the Pregnant Oyster. So we're sitting there in the car, me and this fairly formal businessman who's treating me like a dignitary, and he says to me, 'We have an acquaintance in common. Actually, he's more a relative of mine.' So I ask him, 'Who's that?' and he says, 'My stepbrother is a well-known writer, Peter Weiss.' So this was the stepbrother from the first marriage. Of course, he knew Peter at least as well as I did, but he became a businessman. He told me a lot of things about him, things I hadn't known. For instance, about his passion for the German Romantics, especially Novalis. Then we got to the Kongresshalle and the whole auditorium was full. You always want to know how many people come to my lectures and you're so disappointed when I say there were eighteen, or twenty, or twenty-eight. So this time, I'd never had so many before. This time there were four thousand five hundred people. The mayor of Berlin said some words of welcome to the convention, then all sorts of gentlemen from all over the world spoke, and then it was my turn. I lectured for thirty-five minutes and it turned out to be really good. First I criticized the superficial way they practice their charity, because the conference theme was 'Underdeveloped Man.' By contrast, I made an enthusiastic case for the Berlin students of 1968 and for young people in general. So, I told the gentlemen of the Lions Club that since 1968 mankind had been undergoing a progressive change and they must not interfere with it. Actually, I expected those earnest men to jump all over me in protest, but they were terribly nice. Afterward people came up to me and said, 'We've been coming to this European Forum for years, but thanks to your lecture, Herr Rubin, this was the first time it was really interesting. Peter Weiss's brother was also pleased. In any event, I collected my two thousand marks. I know what you're going to say: I should have asked for at least five thousand. The Lions Club people have a lot of money, but so what? I thought two thousand was completely acceptable. Then Peter's brother took me to the airport and I boarded

a plane for Rome . . . No, first I went to Munich and changed
planes there. Mother was waiting for me when I arrived in
Rome, worried sick of course, as always, because the plane
landed ten minutes late and she was already fearing the worst.
She was really afraid, and maybe there was some reason to be.
In actual fact, I've never experienced such a rough approach
before, except for when Mother flew for the first time, fifteen
or sixteen years ago. That was just as bad. This time, we were
bouncing up and down, up and down, the plane was shaking
something awful—and the funny thing was, it was a Lufthansa
flight, and the pilot didn't say a word. Everybody was sitting
there quiet as a mouse, thinking the end was near, and nobody
in the whole crew told us anything. Usually in such cases they
say, 'We're experiencing some turbulence. Please fasten your
seatbelts,' but nothing of the sort, and that really made everyone afraid. But by the time the pilot started his final approach,
everything was back to normal: 'And now we're landing at
Rome Ciampino.' I spoke to the copilot afterward, and he said,
'I thought it was strange too, but he's the strong silent type,
the captain is.' Anyway, our dear mother had conjured up an
enormous threat in her mind—and perhaps we really were in
danger—but as soon as she saw me, she was in a good mood.
And then the people from the Institute for Nuclear Research
picked us up. They were holding their annual convention near
Grossetto and it took us two and a half pretty unbearable hours
in a big station wagon to get to the place where the conference was. That was still the afternoon of the same day I had
given the speech for the Lions Club people. So we arrived at
eight, eight-thirty, right? But there wasn't any town at all, just

a tourist hotel. Very modern—you know, on the coast, with bungalows. But even though it looked terribly elegant, it was actually quite shabby. Sophia Loren owns the place, but she rents it out. No town nearby—Grossetto was miles away—in the middle of a pine forest constantly patrolled by police, with spotlights on all night long, and a huge, awful ballroom. I was supposed to be the last speaker of the conference the following morning. This was the evening before, and they were having a gigantic party in that ballroom. We weren't expecting any of this at all, and I was terribly tired. But there were a bunch of fine people there—Pestalozzi, Mohl—a lot of people we knew, including that Häsler guy who did that good interview with me. Right off, he did another one with me, this time about science and religion. And then we went to our room, which we didn't like very much. But we finally got to sleep after I had a good deal of difficulty getting the windows blacked out. I got up very early the next morning because I hadn't prepared my speech at all and needed to at least write down some key words. At ten o'clock it was my turn to talk. I improvised, and there was a discussion afterward. By noon everything was basically over. So that was November fifth. Our original plan was to stay and relax a bit until we left for the next conference in Davos, because I thought it would be beautiful there by the sea. But the weather was nasty and the hotel uncomfortable, and they weren't paying for the extra days, so we would have had to pay an awful lot of money to stay in a completely uninteresting place. We decided to stay just one more night, until the sixth, a Sunday, and then we spent a few wonderful days in Rome . . ."

On the main square of Grinzing, near a streetcar stop, an elderly couple approached father and son. The man accosted Ludwig: "How nice to run into you here, Herr Professor Rubin. We are great admirers of yours. Might we ask you for an autograph?" They were from Wuppertal, said that they had been following Father's work for years and fully supported his commitment to protecting the environment. Without the least hesitation, he gave them an autograph, thanked them for their kind words, and was pleased to be recognized and praised. Gustav stood there feeling less visible than a silhouette.

"Allow me to introduce my son," Father said at last. "His name is Gustav and he's a historian." On such occasions, he never said what his son's real occupation was. The friendly couple from Wuppertal nodded at Gustav.

"You must be very proud to have such a famous father!" said the husband and gestured in Ludwig Rubin's direction with the tip of his walking stick.

Gustav nodded. They said good-bye. It had always been like this, ever since Gustav's earliest childhood. Wherever he was, whomever he told his name to, it was always and forever: You're not related to Ludwig Rubin, are you? And as soon as he said yes, or even admitted he was Ludwig's only son, a flood of praise and admiration gushed out over him. He was congratulated, envied for being the child of such a magnificent, important, intelligent man. So you're Ludwig Rubin's son!

"Charming people, both of them. Didn't you think?" Father asked as they resumed their walk.

"So, where was I?"

"Rome. Then you went to Rome . . ."

"So, what can I say, my dearest Burscherle, my Schatzi? We had ourselves driven to the nearest train station, Grossetto. Before that we had some sort of terrible fight, your mother and I. I can't remember what it was about. She made a lot of trouble with the people from the institute. Nothing was right for her. It was just her nerves. She's *exactly* what you've always called her, the woman without a filter! Then we took the train back to Rome. It was so much more pleasant than the ride there by car. Then we took a taxi with all our luggage, piles of suitcases, and drove to Franca's—my friend from younger days. A wonderful lunch, on Sunday, along with her husband Waldo. We toasted our absent children—you and Sabina. Over dessert I pondered what kind of hotel we should stay in. I'd always flirted with the idea of staying in the Hotel de Ville in the Via Sistina, and I thought, let's see if it's really all that much more expensive than other hotels. The price was very reasonable and we had a magnificent room, looking out onto a park, on the sixth floor, right by the Spanish Steps, and easy to black out. We watched the Pasolini film *Arabian Nights*, which isn't very good. But there are some wonderful scenes in it, purely visually: a couple of very pretty girls and a whole lot of you-know-whats. It's got to be the movie with the most—I've hardly ever seen a movie with so many penises in it—close-ups, from the side, from a distance. That's probably how he marketed it, Pasolini I mean. So what else? We spent a lot of time in cafés, and we shopped. There was one unpleasant incident with Mother. It was almost midnight and

we were still sitting in a restaurant not far from the Piazza
Navona. I was awfully tired. But Mother was eating her salad
so slowly it was gruesome, one leaf at a time. I said to her,
'Please, Burschi, don't eat so slowly. I've just got to get to bed.'
So Mother fished all the stuff out of her mouth, the chewed-
up leaves and entire pieces of carrot, more and more of it, out
of her gullet, threw it onto her plate and dumped it onto the
floor of the restaurant! Unfortunately, I had to write my com-
mentary for the radio the next day—there's always something
or other I have to write—and then we flew to Zurich. And
just imagine, the institute had reserved a room for us in the
Hotel Europe—you know it, don't you? that beautiful one in
the Dufourstrasse?—but it was so late, they'd given up on us
arriving and gave the room to someone else. So there was nothing left but a tiny room on the second floor looking out on
the street. And no blackout curtains! We were desperate. We
called ten or fifteen other hotels—all booked up, not a room
to be had. So we decided to stay in the Europe after all, since
we were leaving pretty early the next morning anyway. We
had them bring us some black cloth and I draped all the windows. It took forever. Then we stuck poopies in our ears and
the noise wasn't bad at all, nothing we couldn't live with. Then
in the morning we were on our way again, to Davos, where
there was another very interesting conference. The one near
Grossetto, on the other hand, I could have skipped. I really
didn't need to go; it was just that Italy is such an attraction
that I accepted the invitation. But in Davos it was great. There
were Frenchmen, Israelis, Americans—especially a very good
man from Menlo Park by the name of Berg, a Jew of course.

I gave a big lecture on public science, quite good, I think. At least everyone found it very stimulating. I spoke about the public's relation to science. I had the last lecture again; that seems to have become my specialty. We met some very nice people there, but Davos itself is terribly ugly, not at all reminiscent of *The Magic Mountain*. And then just imagine, it snowed this early in the year, but very wet snow. Just miserable, wet snow . . . very unpleasant. But as I said, we met some people, including Henry Wiener from Santa Barbara, who said I should come visit him there. I plan to go to California soon, as soon as possible. Let me see now—from Davos I went to St. Gallen. Mother went on ahead to Zurich while I gave a talk on solar energy at the adult education center in St. Gallen. A lot of applause, but I'd written that lecture out word for word a few weeks ago so I wouldn't repeat myself. So I read it from the page with a few extemporaneous insertions, and it really was a great success. Afterward six people stayed for a discussion that went on until all hours, about whether it's possible to have imagination. Isn't all imagination just a recombination of old, remembered images? We can't imagine anything we haven't already seen. Isn't it possible that imagination is only a mixture of things we're already familiar with? Can anyone ever find something new, after all, beyond what he already knows? At three a.m. I went to my room. It was ice cold and I started shivering, I was already so overtired. I hit the sack and slept until eight the next morning. Then from St. Gallen back to the Hotel Europe in Zurich, where Mother was waiting for me. We stayed another night there, but this time in a very nice room, and then I said good-bye to Mother early the next morning. She went home alone. She'd had enough, was pretty exhausted. And at nine o'clock I took the train to Stuttgart. You can't imagine how beautiful parts of that route are! My God, the most beautiful meadows—veritable Elysian fields— and forests, and little alpine huts. It must look wonderful in the spring, when everything's in bloom. It had just rained a bit, and then the sun came out and everything looked so fresh! And for miles and miles, not a car in sight, not a single person far and wide in that tremendously lovely landscape. So sometime, I'd definitely like to go hiking there with you, it's so unbelievably beautiful. And fir trees, gigantic firs! When I arrived in Stuttgart . . . What can I tell you? It's a long story. I left a plastic bag at the train station. I'd hidden the money I earned in Switzerland in it. So I had to go back to the station, and I found the bag. It had already been swept into a pile and almost thrown away by the cleaning crew. Please don't tell Mother. Went back into the city, then forgot two other plastic bags—you see what happens when you're overtired. My next event was a seminar in a monastery, three hours' drive from Stuttgart. A photographer was supposed to drive me there along with another participant, Herr Mencke-Glückert. A half hour into the drive, the driver says, 'I'm out of gas. I've got to fill up.' Turns out there aren't any gas stations still open. All closed. We had to turn around, back to the hotel in Stuttgart. We barely made it. Took off at six-thirty next morning, because my lecture was supposed to be at nine. So this time, we're driving for half an hour and then get into the worst snowstorm I've ever witnessed. We drive on for a while. We get to some remote village in the Swabian Alps, and there's a hill the car just can't make it up. It starts to skid, and we get stuck, in the middle of this blizzard, in a village in the middle of nowhere. Where's the nearest phone? I go into a tavern and they tell me they don't have a telephone. The only phone booth in the place is on the village square. We wade through the snow to a tiny train station on a narrow-gauge spur line. (No trace of a phone booth, by the way.) Remember how I used to always strictly forbid you to catch snowflakes in your mouth as a child, on account of the atmospheric atomic tests of the Russians and Americans? I was really afraid of radioactive contamination back then. I was reminded of that, because I was letting the flakes snow into my mouth, I had such an awful thirst, but I had no intention of going back to that awful tavern. We waited half an hour, were starting to think maybe the spur line had been shut down. There was no posted schedule. And then after forty minutes, a little train actually pulls in! One of the last private rail lines in Germany, the Hohenzollern-Sigmaringen Railway. In Sigmaringen we took a cab to the Inzigkofen Monastery. We arrived at noon, completely exhausted. I gave my talk in the afternoon in this marvelous, secluded monastery. Wonderful, beautiful area where no one ever goes, with chalk cliffs and solitary forests and cawing ravens. In the evening I went back to Stuttgart with a fellow from the radio. Stayed in the Hotel Zeppelin again. From Stuttgart to Brussels, for a TV program about me. They really sang my praises, unbelievable. The whole show made me feel like I was already a monument standing on a pedestal. They called me a great humanist, the Erasmus of the twentieth century, stuff like that. What a great hotel room I had in Brussels! Really grand. I could look out over the city toward the train station in the morning, after the sun came up. I was already awake because in the night I'd been too tired to darken the windows, but in November it doesn't get light until relatively late. I have to admit I find this kind of luxury hotel very seductive: taking a bubble bath and then a wonderful breakfast in bed, listening to the radio. I love the evening turndown service in good hotels, when they come to make up the bed again, plump the pillows, smooth the bedspread, and clean the bathroom. You get fresh bath towels and the puddles from your afternoon shower disappear. And there's a good-night candy on the night table! So I'm the Erasmus of the twentieth century . . . Anyway, at the TV station there was this young woman who looked very Jewish and called out 'Hello! Hello!' and gave me a hug. I said, 'I don't know you, do I?' and she answered, 'Doesn't matter!' She was enormously hot, had studied theater in Brussels, and was interning at Belgian Television. So nice, so sincere, very young. What happened then, my sweetheart, you can probably imagine. I was lucky, as always. It was a quickie, a very amusing number. And in Brussels, in that most pleasant of hotel rooms! And yesterday, November tenth, I went to the airport and flew back to Vienna, to Mother. She was already yearning for my return, even after such a short time apart. And so we come full circle. So, now it's your turn, Burscherle. Tell me what you did this past week. Anything interesting since we last parted?"

11

It was announced through bullhorns that the emergency helicopter returning to New York had room for a few extra people,
if there was anyone who wasn't a driver and was having serious health concerns because of the gruesome pile-up. But they
would have to hurry, because the helicopter was about to leave
for the heliport next to the NYU Tisch Hospital on Thirty-
fourth Street. It's like the exodus of that crowd of Americans
and their South Vietnamese employees still in Saigon at the
end of the Vietnam War, thought Gustav. State Department
personnel, businessmen, secret police, secretaries—all on the
roof of the U.S. embassy and fighting each other to be flown
to safety in the very last helicopter. But the association didn't

quite work, because here nobody stepped forward. Gustav caught himself thinking, I'll send Mother! He suggested to Rosa that she take them up on the offer.

"Have you lost your mind? First of all, I won't fly in a chopper. I'm not about to commit suicide. Secondly, I'm going to stay with you. I'm lonely, worn out. And thirdly, I want to be with Father. I can't just leave him lying there all alone. Give me your arm and we'll take a little stroll like I used to with Papa. And then we'll go over and see if we can get a better look at him."

They sauntered along the bridge railing as if on a spa promenade.

"I'm awfully hungry, aren't you?" Rosa inquired. And without waiting for an answer, she continued, "You married the wrong woman. She's dragging you down with her sadness instead of building you up with cheerfulness. But she's incapable of doing that. You would need someone who gives you strength and joie de vivre, like Father gave me. Em steals your courage to face life and makes you melancholy. She always takes and never gives."

He pulled his arm away. "I'm going to pack you onto that helicopter and send you away, Mom, if you don't shut up right now."

"You see, that's the way you react when the other person is right. Otherwise, you'd just laugh it off . . ."

In earlier times, before he'd met Madeleine, Mother used to call up his girlfriends not long after he began a new relationship. Rosa would engage these women, most of whom she'd never met, in conversation about their interests, their career plans, where they were from. She would chatter along cheerily, revealing some of her own life story as well—the escape from Europe, the murder of her parents in a Polish concentration camp—and would make a point of letting them know how famous, world-famous in fact, her husband was. Was the young lady even aware of that? And then, at the very end of the conversation, she'd slip in a friendly warning: unfortunately, my son is an unbelievable liar. He won't make you happy. You'll rue the day you ever met him. Good-bye, and all the best.

A young woman was approaching, her hands thrust into the pockets of her tattered jeans. Gustav asked if she had a cell phone he could borrow for a quick call to a number in New York State. She neither smiled nor answered. A thick braid hung down almost to her tailbone. Her red hair shone in the late afternoon sunlight. Her face and bare arms were sprinkled with freckles.

Rosa repeated the question, "Please forgive us for being so pushy, but—"

Without a word, the woman then pulled a device no bigger than her palm out of her left pocket and handed it to Mother. Mother passed the cell phone to Gustav. He smiled his thanks to the woman—a little too sweetly, it occurred to him—and punched in the number of their vacation home.

Madeleine was standing right by the telephone. In the background, he heard the two children screaming. Julia was crying, while Amadée called out over and over, "I saw you waving! I saw you waving! I can see everything you see, on my computer, but Mommy's so mad at you she won't even take a look!"

Gustav described the current situation on the bridge to his wife.

"You're unreliable, clumsy, and mean," she replied. "How can you let something like this happen? Your mother, of course, is overjoyed to have you all to herself. Am I right?" How often she accused him of being much closer to his parents than to her and the children. Even in the first months of their relationship, she sensed that he was constantly thinking of his parents and not really of her, even when they were making love. In one of her recurring dreams, they were being driven into cattle cars—Gustav, his parents, and his wife. But instead of staying at Madeleine's side, he ran over to his parents and left her all alone. He was pushed into a car with Father and Mother and then stayed with them, while Mad was jammed in with total strangers, far away, in another car. And every time she woke up, she would groan, "It's just lucky we don't have any children yet in my dream . . ." She said that in reality she often felt just as she did in the dream: mercilessly left in the lurch by Gustav.

"Is it my fault that I'm caught in the worst traffic jam of my life?"

"It's never your fault. You're always completely innocent. I've had enough of your stories, I really have. I've been trying to reach you for an hour. What was the problem? Do you have any idea how worried we were?"

"Our battery is dead. I borrowed a cell phone from somebody else—"

"Who were you talking to for so long?"

"Mother was calling Babette."

"I give up. I'm at the end of my rope."

"Me too . . ." He turned the telephone off and gave it back to the woman.

"Cell phones have changed the world," she said, charmingly.

"Aren't you going to thank the nice lady?" Mother asked.

This time the woman smiled. In parting, she confided to them in a low voice, "If you're interested, I'm going to give a kind of seminar back there, near my car. Some people have started preparing little lectures or telling their favorite stories to pass the time. Want to stop by in a while?"

Mother asked what she was going to talk about.

"Just come and listen." And she put her hands back in her pockets. "I was up at the east end of the bridge. The overturned truck has been righted again. It won't be long now."

"And the chemicals that were spilled?" Mother asked.

"I don't know anything about that," replied the young woman. "So, see you later!" And she continued briskly on her way.

"My goodness, wasn't she pretty, really striking. So attractive and innocent," Mother remarked. "Did you notice her lips? They were curved like an Indian's bow. There was something sensual about her, don't you think? Those enormous eyes, and all those freckles . . ."

She would have aroused Father, he thought, even before he realized how much he'd liked her himself. Once at a summer festival in the Salzkammergut, in the lakeside villa of an

Austrian film star, father and son had been attracted to the same woman, an English fashion designer. Her first collection had made her famous all over Europe. She moved with soft gravity, and her serious expression was irresistible. Ludwig and Gustav had prowled around her right in front of Rosa, who was celebrating her sixty-fifth birthday that evening among friends and pretended not to notice. Father and son tried hard to engage the Englishwoman in conversation, to attract—to seize—her attention. It was the first time in Gustav's twenty-nine years of life that he and his father were courting the favors of the same woman. And she was making eyes at both of them. In this one contest, the son defeated the father, managed to extort an address and telephone number from the woman he still didn't really know, went to see her in London a few weeks later, and seduced her on the twenty-third floor of a hotel across from Hyde Park. She promptly got pregnant.

In the eighth week of the pregnancy, she announced, "I have no intention of bearing a child who's related to your mother." On that first evening, in the garden on the shore of the Altausseer lake, she had been watching Rosa out of the corner of her eye. "I couldn't stand your mother from the moment I met her. She's a conceited old witch who's got nothing to say but plays the big shot in public. You should be like your father, not your mother."

"Whatever became of that female you knocked up ten years ago or so . . . or has it been that long?" Mother suddenly asked.

"You're a real mind reader, Mom. I was just this minute thinking about her and what she told me: 'Why don't you just rob a store. Then you'll get into the papers as a thief and not as the son of your famous father. Then you'll be the guy who stole something, and you'll finally be rid of your image as a dutiful, if somewhat colorless, son.'"

"That doesn't answer my question."

"I've lost touch with her. She became a painter and lives outside Dublin. That's all I know."

"How can anybody lose track of a person they were in love with, they slept with, and even almost had a child with? How can that be? People aren't supposed to treat each other like that. How can my own son behave that way? What a shame. You scare me, Burschi."

Clattering loudly, the helicopter swung in a low curve out over the Tappan Zee. They could barely see it, because their view of the sky was obstructed by the rusty superstructure of the bridge.

12

Walking in the trough between two symmetrical waves of metal, the two peaked dragon fins rising up from the steel skeleton like bony spikes, they had reached the middle of the bridge.

Rosa paused to look over the edge. They were standing over Ludwig's navel, which was being washed by the strong current. Because Father was lying on his heart side, his dinner plate-sized navel looked stretched out of shape. How high above the Hudson they were, at least 150 feet above the water! Some distance away, two catamarans could be seen, racing each other.

Gustav was crossing over his father, a special kind of Rubicon experience. Was crossing over him also overcoming him? For a brief instant, it seemed to Gustav that Ludwig Rubin was disintegrating into separate parts down there. The fatherbody: a slaughtered animal the butcher had chopped up into large pieces, into body parts: shank, brisket, chuck steak, short ribs, prime rib, flank steak, and tail. A slaughtered animal, flayed by the furrier and the pelt processed into a stylish man's overcoat. What remained was the skeleton: toe bones, finger bones, and skull here; fibula, patella, coccyx over there; ulna, radius, humerus here; femur and spinal column over there.

He missed not having struggled with Ludwig, that essential phase in the life of a son. He looked so young—much younger than his forty-five years. Whoever hasn't slugged it out with his father, whoever has failed to defend himself will feel weak, incomplete, unmanly the rest of his life—like a chess player unable to defeat a single opponent and gloat in victory, like a knight fallen from his horse in the middle of a joust, like a soldier taken prisoner. You can recognize sons who have not fought this battle by their stooped posture, their constant weariness, their bad mood day and night, their poor digestions. Sons who have not fought this battle are afflicted by all kinds of illnesses. They're as delicate as a mimosa, as vulnerable as a chick fallen from the nest.

Gustav looked down at the fathernavel among the waves. Ludwig David Rubin had been born in Prague, the son of theater people. His mother, Gustav's grandmother, Selly Branden, was appearing onstage until the day before her delivery. The birth was complicated, a premature delivery on Pentecost. The infant was almost strangled by the umbilical cord. It had to remain in an incubator for weeks, although it was already smiling in its first days of life. Since it usually takes two months for newborns to show the first signs of a smile, it was regarded as a miracle baby. Father's father, Theodor Rubin, who enjoyed something of a reputation as an adviser on theater production and author of silent film scripts, organized a small press conference in the hospital and made sure that the Prague tabloids reported on the smiling newborn in the incubator. Grandmother's colleagues, visiting her in her hospital room, applauded the plucky mother enthusiastically.

When the family moved to Berlin, Ludwig's schoolmates called him "Luddy Who Talks About His Mama So Much" because when he was a little boy, his mother, the famous actress, was his only topic of conversation. He considered it a great gift of fate that he remained an only child, and only adults were invited to his birthday parties. Not a single other child ever attended.

Ludwig's parents' house was frequented by famous men and women of the day: politicians, artists, bon vivants; from Fritz Lang to Egon Erwin Kisch, Fritzi Massary to Charlie Chaplin. The composers Egon Wellesz, Erich Korngold, and Ernst Křenek were close friends of Ludwig's mother, sharing Selly Rubin's passion for Beethoven's piano concertos. Frau Rubin's worship of Beethoven culminated in her clapping the name Ludwig on her son, a name the young man came to hate in secret and intended to shed when he reached adulthood. But it never came to that. Although as a young man, Father had

belonged to a Zionist hiking club, in the years after he fled
Berlin he had so deeply absorbed the grammar of assimilation
that he kept his non-Jewish name.

Gustav had grown up in a similar milieu. He got to know,
among others, Ernst Bloch, Herbert Marcuse, Theodor W.
Adorno, Elias Canetti, not through the medium of the printed
page, not in their books or articles, but as flesh-and-blood
guests, in the living room at home or at summer Sunday
lunches shared on shady restaurant terraces. His family also
knew Adorno's Viennese mistress, the diva Lotte Tobias. After
her trysts with Theodor, she would tell Rosa about the little
suitcase where he kept his collection of whips: the small, short
ones; the long, sturdy ones; the soft whips and the hard ones.
Lotte knew them all, because over the years he had beaten her
with every single one of them. Father's admiration for the
works of Gustav Mahler, whose daughter, the sculptress Anna
Mahler, had been his lover when he was a young man, was
reflected in the name he gave his son, thus repeating the same
violation his own mother had committed against him. And
Gustav, in his turn, named his own son Wolfgang Amadée, not
just in honor of Mozart, but even more as a bow to the com-
poser Wolfgang Rihm. He had met him once during the Salzburg Festival, only for a moment, on the fly so to speak, along
with Rosa, in the lobby of the Hotel Österreichischer Hof. He
loved Rihm's *Unbenannt I* from 1986 and *Klangbeschreibung I*,
composed between 1982 and 1987. It was hard to think of a
more Christian name than Wolfgang, and Madeleine had been
very much opposed to giving it to their son. She insisted that
they call him Amadée, which wasn't a Jewish name either, but

at least one she could live with. Nobody ever again called him
Aharon after the circumcision, however.

"What do you think that beauty with the freckles meant about
people holding seminars on the bridge?" Rosa asked. "We
would surely have noticed if anyone was giving a lecture, don't
you think? Papa would have loved to be able to give a talk
about his stuff here on the bridge, or to tell people about his
parents, whom he worshiped so much!"

Ludwig's father and his father's father, thought Gustav.
He didn't answer Mother. She had almost succeeded, as she
so often did with Father, in breaking his chain of thought and
distracting him. Father's mother and the mother of Mother's
mother. Who had they been? Where had they lived? The invisible, endless chain of generations, stretching back deep into
the Middle Ages and determining everything. And much, much
further back, to the beginnings of history and to the ancestors and ur-ancestors long before the beginning of historical
time. They were all reflected in Ludwig's navel, were all
linked to Gustav's navel and the navels of his two children.
One is so ignorant of one's own ancestors: at best, you may
know the dates of your four grandparents, rarely something
about the lives of your eight great-grandparents, and only
under the rarest of circumstances anything at all about your
sixteen great-great-grandparents.

Before Gustav got married, he lived for a while on the top floor
of that shoddy new building on the Danube Canal, in the apartment that Father had once used as an office and stuffed full of

masses of paper that rose like Noah's flood. Whenever Gustav climbed the stairs instead of using the elevator—on Shabbat or when the power went out or when the elevator was being repaired—he thought of the eight floors of the building as the eight decades of life that he measured out for each of them: his father, his mother, and himself. He had long since moved to a single-family house on the edge of Vienna, in Grinzing, not far from the villa where Father had once injured his toe. Every time he found himself in a stairwell, he recalled the eight floors of the apartment building on the Danube Canal. By now, he himself had reached the fourth floor, was already somewhere between the fourth and the fifth. Father had died at the age of eighty-one. Mother would turn eighty-two next year. Would she live for another decade? Would the eighth floor prove to be the top floor of her life as well?

Until her fifties, Rosa was able to convince her son that she was ten years younger than Father. Gustav didn't learn the truth until he was fourteen. His parents were having a fight in a London hotel room. At the climax of the argument, Father yelled, "You are such an unbelievable liar!"

"Me? What do you mean?"

"You even lie to your own child!"

"What are you talking about?"

"He still thinks you're ten years younger than me!"

"How old is Mommy really?"

"Come on, we're leaving!" Father shouted across the double bed to his son. They left the room on the sixth floor of the Hotel Russell at a run and crossed the square. "Hurry up!

We'll catch a bus!" They boarded the first double-decker bus that stopped in Russell Square, the number 36 to Marble Arch, clambered up onto the top deck, and staggered all the way to the front, Gustav's favorite seat, where you feel like you're floating above the streets of the metropolis. There they sat down at last.

"What did you mean about Mommy lying about her age?"

"She was born the same year I was! We were born less than three months apart!"

From then on, Gustav regarded his mother in a different light.

"You're so quiet, Schatzi. Are you starting to get tired after all?" Mother asked. "It wouldn't surprise me. Don't be shy; you can tell me. If you want to, you can lie down in the car, on the back seat, like you did in the Oldsmobile when you were little. Whenever we visited friends or took a spin in the country and were driving back home late at night, you always stretched out on the back seat and went to sleep. Come on, let's go back to the car, Burschi. We'll be on our way again soon, if brooms start flying."

He loved this expression of his mother's: if brooms start flying. As a child, he pictured witches' brooms shooting through the air whenever Rosa said it. He couldn't think of anyone else who said "if brooms start flying," neither in his childhood nor in the present.

"Let's keep going a little. I want to find out if we can see Father's third nipple, the tiny one. It's important to me . . ."

145

"Because it reassures you that you're really his son. He was always a stranger to me, no matter how much I loved him. He was someone I needed, to create my child."

"A stud bull to help you conceive me."

"You always oversimplify everything so terribly."

"I'm just repeating—"

"You made that up. I never said that."

"Just like I made up the story about the prank you played on me when I was ten or eleven. You always deny that too. We were on our way to the grocery store and out of the blue you pretended not to know me anymore. We were in the middle of the sidewalk; I'd just taken your hand. I thought you were joking, even laughed along at first, but you stuck to your guns: 'What do you want from me? Who are you? You are not my son. No, I'm not your mother. Get out of here. Go away, right now!'"

"Will you please stop trying to prove to me how mean I was to you? No mother has ever loved a child as much as I loved you."

"You pulled your hand away when I tried to take it. At the meat counter, where I was usually given a nice thick slice of sausage for free, you told the smirking butcher that some boy had been dogging your heels for ten minutes, claiming to be your son. 'Do you by any chance know who he is?' you asked the butcher. He shook his head, and you replied, 'We've got to do something, Herr Fiala, we can't just leave the child on his own without any parents.' You didn't knock off the joke until I started to cry so hard that all the other customers came running over. And then you acted as if it had all been just a game that I, of course, had taken much too seriously."

"I don't remember that. It's just as absurd as that story about our supposed kissing in bed on Sunday mornings. Meshugge. But as long as we're on the subject, what else are you holding against me?"

"That you pressured me into the wrong profession. I should have listened to Father back then, not to you. But of course, you wanted to keep a connection to your father, a secret connection through me, through my job."

"You should have listened to yourself, not to him or to me. And so? Anything else? Any other reproaches? Just let it all out, let it all out!"

They came to a group standing in a half-circle off to one side of the cars, along the middle divider, where the construction site was. They were listening to a short, elderly lady who was giving an improvised lecture. They caught the words ". . . the airy beauty of suspension bridges," and then she continued in a hoarse voice. "London Bridge existed for six hundred years, carrying shops and living quarters on a tunnel-like street. The fire that destroyed the bridge, in the year 1212, killed eight thousand souls, believe it or not. The greatest bridge builders in history were the Romans. One of their incredible works of art, the Sant' Angelo in Rome, crossing the Tiber, is still standing more than a thousand eight hundred years after it was built. To me, bridges are songs in space. Nowhere on this planet do I feel as spiritually elevated as on a great bridge." Her grayish white eyebrows were so bushy they looked like a man's.

"For heaven's sake, Burschi, you're not going to listen to a speech on the history of bridges, are you?"

"Just for a minute, Mother. Please be quiet . . ."

The woman hesitated momentarily when she heard Rosa's voice, thinking she was addressing her, then she continued. "Primitive man had no interest in building bridges, since they made it rather too easy for his natural enemies to follow his trail. Let us keep in mind that the safety of isolation offered by water was eliminated by the bridge—"

"You always lump everything together—me, your father, your marriage, and your family life—and now you insist on listening to this frightful bore as well."

"For primitive man, water meant protection. There's an old superstition that no demon, ghost, or supernatural body can cross running water—"

"So, I'm going to keep on going," Rosa informed her son. "You can do as you please!"

"Caesar and Napoleon were the world's most important bridge builders before the modern age. They of course needed bridges for their military conquests. And who were the most important bridge builders of the modern age? I will tell you who, and I am proud to be a descendant of theirs: the Roeblings, father and son: John Augustus Roebling and Washington Roebling, the builders of the Brooklyn Bridge over the East River, less than thirty miles from here, once considered the eighth wonder of the world!"

"Are you coming or not?" Mother called to her son from some distance away.

She would always interrupt Father just like this when he was in the middle of a conversation. She'd tug at his sleeve, saying he shouldn't bother with such unimportant, uninteresting individuals (fellow researchers, journalists, politicians), shouldn't waste his time with trivialities. And Father would fly into a rage, berate Mother for her ignorance and lack of curiosity, her intellectual laziness and narrow-mindedness, which he attributed to the fact that she was a star dancer in her childhood and youth and later toured the provinces as an operetta soubrette instead of going to school and getting a proper education. Whenever she didn't know something, her standard excuse was "I was absent from school the day they covered that." Gustav couldn't recall ever seeing Rosa with a book in her hand. It wasn't her thing to sit in an armchair or on a sofa and read. She had to have the telephone to her ear or the news blaring from the radio or the TV. She never played a classical record, never listened to a sonata, a piano concerto, or a symphony, not even for a quarter of an hour.

Father always resented the fact that Mother had no profession and no job of her own. His temper tantrums would always culminate in the shrill admonition, "Do something!" He told her she was a know-it-all who corrected every step he took, but it never occurred to her to do anything herself. "And I don't just mean earning money, not at all. It's not so important that you don't contribute to our income, but you lead a completely inactive life—it's insufferable and I can't understand it. I just can't comprehend how anyone can live the way you do. You spend your days like a swan, a seagull, a duck—with no goal in mind! With absolutely nothing to do. Do something!"

When Gustav was a child, Mother's ignorance would completely exasperate him. And yet she was wondrously successful in acting as though she knew what was going on, as though nothing was unfamiliar to her. There was no room for being mistaken in her image of herself. Her fatuity was paired with finesse, her ignorance and lack of education with utmost shrewdness. She knew what excuses would compensate for her errors and mistakes. She was the world champion at inventing excuses. And every time she committed a particularly gross faux pas, she said, "Come on, don't be silly, I was only joking!"

She came back to Gustav, pulled at his sleeve, and moaned, "Will you please leave this old hag to her lecture on suspension bridges and come with me?"

Gustav interrupted the woman's monologue to ask how it was possible for her to say she was a descendant of the builder of the Brooklyn Bridge.

Mother rolled her eyes and seemed close to tears.

"A very good question, sir," replied the lady, pleased to be asked. "I am Washington Roebling's second cousin thrice removed. My great-grandmother was actually a Roebling!" And she proceeded to describe the unusual circumstances under which the Brooklyn Bridge had been constructed from 1869 to 1883, spoke of the astonishing challenge of anchoring the towers, which are as tall as skyscrapers, in the muddy bottom of the East River, explained how men worked in the caissons, the immense chambers that were slowly lowered to the bottom and served as the basis for the later bridge piers, the caissons in which, they said, time passed faster than in the outside world.

"If you don't come right now, Burschi, you're so mean and thoughtless that I'm going to go back on the first train tomorrow morning!"

"To quote a beautiful sentence spoken by the mayor of Brooklyn on the day the Brooklyn Bridge was dedicated," the woman with the bushy eyebrows continued, "'Whoever sees it will feel deep pride in being human!' Isn't that lovely? Every bridge is a floating miracle. God gave us hands to build bridges, for He can't do it himself. Is there a sadder sight than a bridge destroyed by war or natural disaster? Wrecked bridges are like slaughtered cattle. In three millennia of civilization, bridges—the souls of the cities and the countryside—are one of the most noble achievements of mankind. How I love them, these structures of iron that span the water, magnificent silhouettes!"

"I'm leaving now!" Mother called out, much louder than before.

He trotted along behind her as he had once trotted behind his father. His willpower had been imprisoned, frozen in a sort of Sleeping Beauty slumber since his childhood. Otherwise, how could he have ever given up his studies, left his life's path at a decisive fork in the road, and slipped into the role of a pelt monger?

He gave in.

He did what was expected of him.

He let her have her way.

Father had once known how to encourage his son. But Gustav didn't possess the determination or the ambition or the strength to draw sustenance from that encouragement. Ludwig and Gustav Rubin had reversed roles: the sensitive, educated father, interested in philosophy and art, active and vigorous, hugely famous, a cult figure among members of the student movement; the son: an obscure historian, area of specialization the Hundred Years War, weary, enervated, always pale, living out his life as a furrier, an occupation he liked less with each passing year. Although Father considered his son's choice of profession insane, he did feel a touch of gratification that his son's name was not likely ever to outshine his own. Ludwig David Rubin? Aren't you the famous historian's father? That danger had been averted. Gustav Robert Rubin would never become someone who made a name for himself.

His parents' longing for grandchildren was reason enough for him to get married. Did his marriage to Madeleine accord with his own innermost wishes? He could no longer say for certain. He could no longer say anything for certain. He loved his two children, there was no doubt about that. He would allow himself no indecisiveness on that point. Did he love his children sincerely, unconditionally? Wolfgang Amadée and Julia—did they love their father?

"I knew you'd come along after me. Do you remember how Father was always giving interviews when we took that boat from New York to Europe with you in 1960? The journalists came aboard before we sailed, came into our cabin, because it was the year his book *Fusion* appeared. You sat next to him through all the interviews and really got a huge kick out of it. Of course, you were proud of him. Me too, by the way, of course. And how! *Fusion* was published in twelve languages. Or was it seventeen?"

So proud was Rosa of her husband that both before and after his death she always referred to herself, and insisted that others refer to her, as Mrs. Ludwig Rubin.

Not only did Gustav remember the marathon of interviews in the early Sixties, he carried within him memories of a thousand other interviews Father had given in his presence or in his absence but with his knowledge. With each interview Father gave, his son felt a tiny bit weaker, a little more feeble. Every time the grown-up Gustav spoke to Father on the telephone and Ludwig told him where he was traveling to next and what obligations he had to meet in the near future, Gustav felt a degree more helpless, more powerless. Father boasted all the more: "Next week I've got to go to Rome for a TV interview, then to Paris. Three radio stations are clamoring for me. I could be in a different city every day if I wanted to, but now I'm going to stay with Mother in Vienna for four days. You have no idea how many engagements I've already canceled this year! For Mother's sake, but also so I don't completely overstress myself. On the other hand, I can't sit at home all the time!" And then he would continue his list: energy conference in Stockholm, reception at the White House, research trip to four countries in South America, a documentary film being made about him in Berlin. The BBC had once produced a one-and-a-half-hour show in the course of which they also interviewed Rubin's son and only child. "What do you want to be some day?" the filmmaker asked the eighteen-year-old. Gustav stammered, talked about his interest in history and his passion for photography. For a young man of his age, he made a surprisingly childish impression, so indecisive, that that was probably why in the finished film nothing remained of him but a small black-and-white snapshot as a three-year-old with a balloon in his hand, sitting between his parents, taken in the dining room of the *France* during a transatlantic crossing.

Gustav looked at his watch—five p.m. The light was simultaneously harsh and milky, the air almost unbearably hot and humid. He began to think about the fact that he might eventually not be able to spend the coming night in his vacation house. What would he do if Shabbat began before he could get off the bridge? Should he reserve a hotel room for himself just in case, in Tarrytown, on the east side of the Tappan Zee?

An Orthodox couple were sitting in one of the cars. In their closed, creamy beige Chevrolet Impala, they looked as if they were drowning, slipping slowly to the bottom of the river in their car, with no hope of surviving. The woman wore a blond wig and constantly swiveled her head in all directions. The man had long, stringy sidelocks. He struck the steering wheel rhythmically with the palm of his long-fingered hand. Both were very young, possibly still childless. Deep in their bones, they felt the fear of not being where they were supposed to be when Shabbat began at sundown. You could see it in their eyes, like the fear of death.

13

Whenever Gustav stood in the middle of a bridge and looked down, it was the same as when he was a child: he felt as though he were standing at the bow or the stern of an ocean liner, looking down into the churning water as the boat put out to sea. He had stood on so many bridges—arched, girder, suspension, cable-stayed, and cantilever—floating high above the water and feeling as if he were circumnavigating the globe!

But this time, it was completely different: he was afraid. He feared that the Tappan Zee Bridge would collapse under the prolonged load of hundreds of cars, buses, house trailers, motorcycles, livestock trucks, motorboats and sailboats in tow, plus the weight of many hundreds of travelers. The bridge rested on innumerable pillars, yet seemed to him in acute danger. Gustav, the only son of an eminent physicist, couldn't comprehend, either, why an airplane packed with 350 passengers and all their heavy possessions and suitcases didn't fall from the sky. He didn't understand how radio waves, television broadcasts, Internet traffic, or telephone connections worked. But of course he acted as if he did.

He thought back to his childhood, could see himself in Vienna on the Bruckner footbridge, which he had crossed every day on his way to and from school. It was at the time his parents had left America to settle in Vienna and before they moved back to Los Angeles. The wooden and iron pedestrian bridge over the Wien River had been built a hundred years earlier. It was a half-timbered bridge, and from it he could see his parents' apartment on the top floor of a building on the edge of the Stadtpark, its windows illuminated golden yellow in the evening. Thirty years had gone by since then, but even at the time, Gustav knew: someday I will cross this bridge and look up at the lighted windows and strangers will be living in that apartment—a painful vision of the future that had tortured him every day.

He was worried about Mother. She was leaning against the railing and suddenly looked pale and exhausted and years older. She should sit down and rest. He reproached himself for taking her so far from the car.

"Mother?"

"Yes?"

"Let's go back to the car."

"Why?"

"Because you're . . . tired."

"Because we're tired."

"OK, because we're tired. And because we're hungry and thirsty."

"First I want to take a closer look at Father's belly. We're almost there."

"But then we'll go straight back to the car."

"If that's what you want . . ."

Father's abdomen was the size of a soccer field and bulged out into the current. How he had suffered from abdominal and stomach pain! He was hardly ever able to enjoy a meal without suffering distress afterward. He took medications every day—before meals, after meals, always new ones and more and more of them. Some made him drowsy. Others made him so wide awake they kept him up all night. Some made him depressed and some had no effect at all. Once or twice a year, he went to a health spa, usually alone, to spare Mother the torture of having to watch him struggle to follow the prescribed regimen and submit to the periodic examinations he hated. For ten to fourteen days, he would seal himself off from the outside world and subject himself to the strictest nutritional regulations at ever-changing locations, in clinic after clinic, in Austria, Switzerland, Italy, or Romania. But as soon as he returned from these orgies of self-denial, he would begin to suffer again just as much as before.

"I regard these dreadful pains I have to put up with after every meal as just punishment," Ludwig informed his son, sitting in the dining room of a Styrian gastrointestinal clinic with walls papered in gray. "No, Gustav, not punishment—that's the wrong word. But as the price I have to pay for the marvelous life I get to lead. My only regret is that I could never travel to India on account of my stomach, that I have to pick the raisins out of a Gugelhupf before I eat it, even though raisins are my favorite food. All the things I'm allowed to eat have absolutely no taste at all!" (Neither his irritable bowel nor his delicate stomach, however, would cost Father his life. A tiny blood clot would lodge in his brain and cause the stroke.)

Every single day of his adult life, Ludwig spent endless sessions in the bathroom, armed with the newspapers and magazines he subscribed to. People spend a third of their lives asleep. Father, however, spent a good tenth of the remaining two-thirds in the john. When the victorious warrior emerged, he was able to enjoy a few hours of peace, a short interval without pain, sweet moments of boundless satisfaction with himself and the world.

Especially at meals, they would often think he was lost in thought or preparing a lecture in his mind, looking for fresh formulations to make his newest scientific discovery comprehensible to the general public. But he was only listening inwardly to the convulsions in his stomach and bowels. "I'm like the character in that Joseph Conrad novel," he would say. "You should read it some time—I think it's *Lord Jim*, but I'm not sure. But the two of you never read anything anyway. What a shame; it's a wonderful story. The crew thinks that the captain is constantly in a foul mood, but he's just listening to his own innards because he has dreadful stomach pains, just like me." All the doctors Father consulted confirmed the diagnosis: he was suffering from the chronic gastritis he had contracted at the age of thirteen by draining that entire bottle of vinegar as a test of courage.

Father's intestinal wind had attended Gustav's childhood like a constant storm. Whenever he slipped into his parents' bed on Sunday morning, the powerful clouds of gas that had accumulated beneath the blankets overnight were suddenly released into the stuffy air of the bedroom. Yet even in midsummer, the blacked-out windows always remained closed to block out the street noise, however minimal it might be.

"If anything should ever happen to me," Ludwig told Gustav about ten years before his stroke, his voice ringing with the conviction that nothing at all could happen to him—he never spoke of his own end, wouldn't allow the word "death" to be spoken, wouldn't let anyone talk to him about dying— "then just remember: I've had a fantastic life. I've enjoyed every minute of it. Never forget that, never! Promise? And I don't always have to drain every cup to the last drop. Just the possibility of an experience is often enough for me—just the fact that it's all out there. Sometimes a glance into a café, bar, or restaurant terrace, the sight of a young woman—especially in Italy—is enough for me to be able to fill in, imagine the entire experience. I can envision it for myself, definitively. I love life so much, Gustav. Every minute is worth living, every minute." They were sitting in the regional train from Genoa to Santa Margherita Ligure during one of their hiking trips when Ludwig said this in a way his son had rarely ever heard from him before. They had eaten like kings next to the harbor, drunk ice-cold pinot grigio, and then walked to the train station on unsteady legs and departed the city on the first train that showed up. In that same regional train, Father had spoken of his fury that after one dies, the world stays the same and life continues on as before. When an individual dies there's nothing to mark his death: not a single hair lies differently on the head of a child, not a single building collapses, no river reverses direction, no cherry tree blooms more slowly. After one's disappearance, everything stays as it is, imperturbable and unchanging.

Until his eightieth birthday, in all his thoughts and actions, in his addiction to more and more and more of whatever was the newest fad, Ludwig always seemed to be by far the younger of the two of them. He was more lively than his students, more alert than ambitious young artists, more optimistic than most people at the beginning of their careers. He worked every day from early in the morning until late at night, writing, reading, discussing, analyzing. Only on Sunday—but never on Shabbat—did he sometimes observe a day of rest. His consumption of paper would have done honor to the editorial staff of a major metropolitan daily. Ideas were constantly occurring to him—"ambushing me," as he put it—even at an advanced age. "I get my best ideas in the mountains, going downhill!" In the cities where he resided he could often be seen hurrying through streets and alleys with a cassette recorder in one hand, registering a new thought every thirty seconds with the device held close to his lips. In the course of his life, he had misplaced a huge number of voice recorders, bought new ones, lost them again, dropped them on the ground. Their forward and reverse mechanisms, record buttons, and replay functions got jammed, their batteries leaked and ruined them for good. But the number of devices that he used until they simply stopped running was also huge. After he was buried, cassette recorders they had thought lost forever were discovered in drawers, bookcases, coat pockets, and plastic bags, in small suitcases and carry-ons, some damaged but others fresh from the factory—dozens of them.

He would suffer bouts of exhaustion that always took him by surprise, but after only ten minutes of yawning himself out, he would have overcome them. "How can I be so tired?" he wondered. After half a century of unceasing hard work, he railed like a person upset by an inscrutable fate. (He followed a daily regimen that was so strange, no one else would be able to comprehend it, but he maintained an impressive, persistent diligence. Without making a big deal of it, and with matter-of-fact humility, he was a hard worker.)

Gustav strove to emulate his father's energy, but he didn't possess it, and he envied him for it. And as he envied him his energy, he also envied him his imagination, his amiability, his kindness, the forcefulness of his personality. Ludwig had a quick temper, but it was outweighed by his kindness. That was his defining characteristic. It was the secret power of his being and the reason he willingly allowed anyone and everyone to get close to him—be they good or evil, fascinating or boring, sane or insane. It was not just curiosity motivating his openness, but his deep commitment to and love for the species *Homo sapiens*.

Father's fantastic, everlasting capacity for hope, his unbearable kindness, completely robbed his son of confidence. Ludwig's immense productivity often rendered Gustav powerless. The more enterprising the father, the quieter and more worn out the son.

The sound of a foghorn tore Gustav from his stream of thought. Its deep drone went on for a long time. It wasn't a car honking or a truck's air horn. Where was it coming from? Was it a sign the traffic jam was about to end? Again, the same deep drone. The stranded drivers looked inquiringly at each other. Then two little twins in pink swimsuits pointed down to the river. Gustav was alarmed. Had the children discovered the father-body? But in that same instant, he realized the source of the honking noise: a small excursion boat was on its way upstream, probably heading for Poughkeepsie, Kingston, or Albany. Three hours had gone by since the beginning of the backup. In that entire time, not a single ship, canoe, rowboat, or tug had passed under the bridge. Up to that moment, it had not even occurred to mother or son that there was ship traffic on the Hudson.

Loud hip-hop reached Gustav's ear from the excursion boat. It was a shrill female group and he couldn't tell if they were on board, performing live. Men and women could be seen dancing on the deck. Suddenly they broke off their convulsions and pointed with outstretched arms to some obstacle that seemed to impede their forward progress. Father was bringing shipping on the Hudson to a halt. There was no possibility of the boat swerving toward the east or west bank. The water would have been too shallow there. Gustav and Rosa feared that droves of people would now look down and catch sight of Father's naked body. Even if no one would know who the oversized dead man was, they were nevertheless terribly embarrassed to expose their vulnerable, naked Ludwig to the stares of thousands of people.

Could it be that people on the boat could see what was blocking their way? Even from a distance, their faces and gaping mouths looked frightened, showed evidence of dread and revulsion. But from the bridge people didn't seem to notice that almost all the boat passengers were pointing at Father. Up on the bridge, they probably thought the startled expression of the excursionists had to do with the truck accident and the extreme traffic jam on the Tappan Zee Bridge. The boat was already beginning to turn smartly, gave two more blasts of its deep horn, and made its way full speed ahead back down the Hudson toward Manhattan.

Some passengers were assembled on the stern of the little boat. Gustav could clearly see them staring at Father's titanic nakedness, his majestic immobility—the river god Ludwig David Rubin.

14

"You were right, I can't go on. I'm really feeling very worn out all of a sudden. To tell the truth, I'm a little dizzy," Mother groaned.

"And I've never been as tired in my entire life as I am today."

"But at the same time, you're enjoying this unbearable situation we've gotten ourselves into. You think it's exciting—amusing, even—that a boat turned back on account of us, so to speak, but for me all of this is just terribly embarrassing. For you, of course, an event of such magnitude is a welcome adventure. In the normal course of things, nothing—or very little—ever happens to you, except for a couple of ladies coming upstairs to your store and prancing around in front of the mirror like aging wind-up dolls. Or an occasional burglary, usually perpetrated by your own employees. What exciting stories! And meanwhile, you get richer by the hour without having to lift a finger."

"At the moment, Mother, I'm too exhausted to fight with you, but I will respond to that later."

"I can hardly wait to hear it!"

She didn't have a clue. Even Madeleine knew nothing about the fact that Gustav had been in debt for the past year. Lately, it was becoming increasingly clear that their business was in a slump. The balance sheet of the firm Lichtmann & Rubin had been in the red since the year before last. Gustav's bank account in Vienna had accumulated a considerable deficit. Unlike his partner, who had been transferring assets abroad since he was a young man, Gustav had no numbered accounts in Switzerland. Not the least of his problems was the purchase of the house on Lake Gilead, which had gotten him into the worst financial straits of his life. He had made this investment at a time when the fur business was considerably more healthy, the great worldwide anti-fur campaign of the late Nineties had not yet gathered its full strength, but especially when the firm of Malis & Co. in the Kärntnerstrasse had not yet flooded the market at dumping prices and still had had a long way to go to become the market leader.

"We're losing our skins," Richard Lichtmann tried to joke as the crisis became more and more acute. To cover his most urgent bank debts at least temporarily, Gustav borrowed money from his partner, sums he was unable to pay back. He lay awake at night, feeling a gnawing void in his belly, his chest, a gigan-tic, black hollowness nibbling at the edges of his heart and sap-ping all his energy. For months, he had been afflicted with harrowing depression.

Mother had control of the money Father had left. She didn't give Gustav a cent of it. On the contrary, she wasted it, gave it to Babette, to artists she didn't even know, to an orga-nization for the protection of people harmed by air traffic. She was so generous with her money because she assumed her son possessed much more than she did anyway and lived like Croesus. From time to time she even considered hitting Gustav up for a loan. He, on the other hand, was much too proud to ask Rosa for help. He was ashamed of having gotten himself into this mess, absolutely did not want to reveal to her the extent of his financial catastrophe, not least because he feared her derision. This would never have happened to my father, she would have responded. He knew how to do business! He knew how to handle money!

"At last there's something happening in your life," Mother now forged ahead, "but for me, the whole affair on this accursed bridge is very, very unpleasant. I can't go on; it's used up my last ounce of strength. I know I'm just imagining it all, but then why did that boat turn around? And why did some of the people I asked a little while ago also see somebody lying down there. Come on, let's go. Can't we please finally go back to the car? I've got to sit down or even better, lie down. Ten minutes ago you were suggesting taking me back yourself."

"Just hang in there for a minute, then I'll go back with you. There are moments in life you just can't interrupt."

"Father's third nipple is more important to you than my well-being?"

"Mother, please. Don't be like that!"

She turned and left, walking quickly and energetically in the opposite direction.

A flock of large gulls flew over the bridge. They came from the north, flying south on wide wings, white and beautiful. The whole sky had turned gray. Huge cumulonimbus clouds were rising in the east. The air had become heavy and sultry, as if a thunderstorm were approaching.

Gustav looked longingly in the direction of Father's chest, imagining the solar plexus deep within Ludwig's belly, node of the emotions, gathering place of nerve endings. How often had Father warned him that the solar plexus was the main reason why you shouldn't jump into cold water on a full stomach when you're overheated. When your breathing suddenly becomes labored, a full stomach increases the pressure on the plexus and you lose your voice, depriving you of your last chance to scream for help. You drown.

Ludwig's right arm lay in the water at a contorted angle, like the arm of a drowning man. Everything was magnified a hundredfold: the sparse white hairs, the liver spots, the moles. His right hand, lying near his belly, was clenched in a boulder-sized fist. His left hand, like his left arm, was out of sight.

Father's hand always felt warm when you clasped it. Gustav's hands, however, were always cold. Cold hands and a hot heart, Father had taught his son. But even as a child, Gustav had asked if that didn't also mean hot hands and a cold heart. You may be right, Sonny Boy, my little treasure. Perhaps I'm not as completely noble as I pretend to be, not as sympathetic as I act, not as loving as I seem.

He called him Boychick, beloved Boychick, right up to the end. He would say, My son, you are a wisp of fog. And every time Gustav replied, But Papa, how can you say that? I'm not a wisp of fog! I'm a happy child, aren't I? Ludwig would persist, *Mein Sohn, du bist ein Nebelstreif!* It was a saying he had picked up from his own father, whose favorite poem was Goethe's "Erlking": My son, why hide your face in fear? Father, don't you see the Erlking? The Erlking with his crown and robe? My son, it is a wisp of fog. . . .

Another saying inherited from Grandfather's habits of speech was "not just right away, but right a wrong!" Whenever they were in a particular hurry, or if Ludwig was willing to fulfill a request quickly, he would say, I'll do it not just right away, but right a wrong! And sometimes in the middle of a conversation, when his son would forget what he was about to say and search dispiritedly for the dropped thread, Father always came out with his own father's line: Why don't you just say something similar?

Gustav's gaze rested on Father's right hand, sprinkled with large liver spots. He saw himself on late Sunday mornings or on holidays, playing coin bocce with Ludwig while waiting for Mother. It was his favorite game next to building dams. It always took Rosa an eternity to put on her makeup and get dressed before they drove to lunch at the garden restaurant Zur Schönen Aussicht on the Pfarrplatz in Heiligenstadt. They would stand there on the sidewalk, waiting for Mother to come down at last, in front of their apartment block in the Bayerngasse, which ran parallel to the Beatrixgasse on the edge of Modena Park in the third district of Vienna. Each of them had six or seven coins in his hand, of various sizes and weights, from the feather-light five-groschen coin to the much larger and almost heavy ten-schilling piece. The point of the game was to toss the coins so they landed as close as possible to a target coin about fifteen yards away, the same way you try to bowl bocce balls as close as possible to the *pallino*. They could play their favorite game endlessly, without ever tiring of it. When Mother finally showed up, they were disappointed to have to break it off. And then every time, every single time, Rosa would complain, So I could have taken much longer!

Father's hands—how clumsy they were. They dropped everything, but especially the most beautiful, most expensive plates, bowls, cups, glasses. His hands never repaired, cooked, stirred, or peeled anything. Never in his life would it have occurred to him to sew a button on a shirt, and if it ever had, the undertaking would have certainly ended in failure. It was unthinkable for him ever to have prepared a hard-boiled egg, a piece of meat, or a salad. Mother often hid his keys when he left the house in the morning so that she could control when he was in the apartment and when he wasn't. She emphatically forbade him to be at home by himself, for fear that he might set the catastrophically messy kitchen on fire while putting on a kettle to make himself some instant coffee or a cup of tea.

All the more surprising, then, was another image the son connected with his father's hands: the clatter of Ludwig's typewriter, the noise that dominated his childhood. Father was always sitting at his typewriter, a big, black one with keys on the ends of long steel shafts. A piano with letters. A millipede with characters on all its feet. It didn't matter if Gustav was talking to Ludwig or drawing on the floor or playing with Legos or blocks, Father wouldn't let it disturb him. He just typed and typed at furious speed. At typing he was as adroit as a magician. And while he typed, he smoked without inhaling—just puffed—and as soon as a pack of cigarettes was empty, he tossed it to Gustav to play with, as one tosses a scrap to a pet. The typewriter's clatter was the accompaniment to Gustav's childhood. He heard it when he woke up; he heard it when he went to sleep. And Father typed at sensational speed, with ten fingers, faster than he could speak. Perhaps even faster than he could think.

When Ludwig lay motionless in his hospital bed, felled by the stroke, Gustav brought the typewriter into his room, hoping to lift his spirits. Ludwig looked at it and it even seemed to his son that he smiled for a moment. One morning, months after his paralysis had begun, he made a clumsy movement and fell out of bed. The team of doctors and nurses reacted with panic, more concerned than ever about his well-being. On the afternoon of the same day, however, he had them bring him the typewriter, and he began to type. He seemed to be overjoyed to hear the sound of typing once more. He typed numbers, letters, punctuation marks, without any spaces in between. And when the bright jingle rang out at the end of a line, he kept on typing. He no longer knew he had to use the carriage return to advance to the next line. He completely ignored all the keys on the left side of the keyboard. He had lost his left field of vision in the stroke. Gustav could call out, "Left! Don't forget the keys on the left!" as much as he liked, but Ludwig never got beyond the middle of the ranks of letters. The *A* and the *E*, the *W* and the *B*, the *T* and the *R* remained untouched. But he typed and typed, uncommonly pleased with the clatter of the keys.

Gustav tore himself away from the railing.

He followed after Mother, felt it his duty to stay with her, couldn't let her return to the car by herself.

Whether in town or in the country, how Father had hated coming back from a walk or an errand by the same way he had gone. One must never return by the same path! There was no turning back. Turning around meant a setback, stagnation, the nearness of death. Father always wanted to go forward, nowhere but forward. His goal was the future. Even the present moment was far from his mind. Memory is regress, retreat. I won't return by the same path I came on. I intend to free myself from all retrospection. Ludwig had repeated this like a magic formula his whole adult life.

But how could you return along a bridge deck other than to take the same path in the opposite direction?

Where the expert on bridges had earlier been holding her lecture about the construction of the Brooklyn Bridge and the father–son team of the Roeblings, there now stood a man over six feet tall, pointing toward the south with huge hands. "My tribe settled here some five hundred years ago. We Tappan Indians were a great nation," he declared to the seven people who were listening. "We believed in demons, and we believed in ghosts. The river amidst the high hills meant livelihood, food, and beauty in the shadow of tall walnut trees . . ."

"You're going to stop again and listen to that? He's just drunk, the poor man, can't you see that? First of all, I have to go to the bathroom again, and second of all, I absolutely have to have some coffee or I'm going to faint."

". . . yet we all were massacred in 1881, butchered by Colonel Fred Jones's troops, not too far from here. Four men and three women lived to tell the tale of the slaughter. I am one of the children—or should I say great-great-grandchildren —of those few survivors. Only some three thousand descendants still call themselves Tappan Indians, and many of us have settled around here, near this bridge named after our forefathers."

The Indian did in fact seem a bit tipsy. It may well have been that he had drunk too much. But Gustav was curious, hoped to learn something about the Tappan tribe after whom the Dutch explorers and later the settlers had named the vicinity around the bridge, choosing the word *Zee* because the Hudson at this point was as wide as a lake.

Mother tugged at his sleeve.

She pulled him away.

15

Rosa was the first to reach the Cadillac. Someone had broken into the locked car. Gustav had with him his cash, the little camera, and the cell phone with the dead battery, but his credit cards, driver's license, passport, and return ticket were gone. Mother's purse, containing her wallet with two hundred dollars and her bottle of Chanel No. 5, lay untouched on the passenger seat. He was insured. The rental car company would replace almost everything. He didn't have enough strength left to get especially excited about the burglary.

"You're a nation of crooks! Who did this?" Mother shouted at the people in the vicinity in her strong accent. "Someone must have been watching while this happened! You cowards! Come forth and confess!" A few people standing nearby couldn't suppress their grins, while others tried to calm her down.

No one had noticed the break-in. Nobody could supply them with any further details.

One young woman paid more attention to Mother than the others. It was the freckled woman who had loaned them her telephone an hour ago.

"What can I do for you?" she asked.

"There's so terribly much you can do for us I don't even know where to begin," Rosa replied. "For instance, I need a good strong espresso. I need a nice clean bathroom. We should let my daughter-in-law know that it's going to be a while yet. And many other things. You're charming. Thank you."

"My mother is as old—sorry, as young as you are, and you even look a little like her," remarked the stranger.

"Is your mother as beautiful as I am, too? Are her eyes as intensely blue as mine? Is your father still alive? Do you have any siblings? What's your name? What do you do for a living? Why are you being so nice to us?"

"Mother, please! Too many questions all at once!"

"If this young lady is really as enchanting as I thought when she let us use her phone, then she'll answer all my questions, one after another. And another thing: you said you were going to give some sort of seminar, I don't know about what. How did that go?"

"No one came to hear me."

"But we're listening now, my son and I!"

"I grew up in this area and I planned to give a little talk about it. About the local landscape, the people, and the history of the region," began the young woman. "My mom, Josephine Tassel, brought me up by herself. I've never met my father. My mother's eyes are the same color as yours, the exact same brilliant light blue. Stars of the soul, those eyes, as powerful as the sun. I have no siblings. Maybe some half-siblings, but I don't know them. In any event, my mother had only me. She lives on the other side of the river. If you like, we could pay her a visit together, as soon as this catastrophe here is over. The area around the Tappan Zee is enchanting. Believe me, I know my way around here. There's nowhere else you can see so many falling stars and meteoroids, nowhere in the whole world. What else did you want to know from me?" She had such a winning smile that Gustav's heart started to beat precariously. "My name is Erin," she added.

"And I'm Rosa Rubin. My maiden name was Fuchs," Mother informed the young woman. "My father was a fur dealer in Vienna and my son is continuing in the same business. My husband died just barely a year ago. He was very famous. Ludwig Rubin—perhaps you've heard the name? No? He was a sort of philosopher, but he was also a physicist and nuclear scientist and a bad poet and sometimes, way back when I first met him, a science reporter. And he was a wonderful person and husband and father. I loved him very very much." She paused for a long time before continuing. "And this is my son Gustav. He was very often ill as a child, an enormously affectionate, sweet boy I fed from the bottle until he was three years old. You can't imagine how sweet he was as a baby! And he was eleven before he knew how to spread his own bread. But now he's big, very big even, as you can see. Married, unfortunately—no, I'm not allowed to say that or he gets mad. Anyway, he's a husband and the father of two children. He lives in Vienna and arrived in New York today on a flight that was enormously delayed."

"Not on American Airlines flight 344 from London to JFK?" Erin Tassel looked at the two of them in astonishment.

"How did you know that?" Gustav felt dizzy.

She laughed. She laughed more heartily, more refreshingly than Mother or Madeleine could ever have managed to laugh. It was so pleasant. So liberating. So warm. Did Father have a hand in this meeting? Father? Can you hear me? Gustav whispered in the direction of the bridge railing.

"I know that," said Erin, still grinning, "because I . . . arrived late too, on the same plane."

"What a coincidence! Isn't that funny, Gustav? I absolutely love stories like this. It makes me forget, at least for the moment, how boring life is."

"The outside engine on the left side stopped working," continued the young woman, "three hours after takeoff. Sorry about that."

"Why should you be sorry?" Mother and Gustav didn't understand.

Erin laughed again, or was she *still* laughing? "It really wasn't my fault. Something like that happens once in three thousand flights. You basically can't prevent it, even with the best maintenance."

At that moment, wild honking and cheering broke out to the east, at the far end of the bridge, a jubilation like one you might hear in a dream. They guessed immediately that the huge obstacle had been removed. The traffic jam was already slowly beginning to break up in the distance. In a quarter of an hour it would all be over.

Erin moved toward her car, a blood-red Grand Am that could have been the twin of the model mother and son had exchanged in Manhattan.

"Just a moment, if you please. You can't arouse our curiosity to this extent and then simply dissolve and disappear." Rosa wasn't about to give up. "Tell us why you're laughing in such a strange, mischievous way. You're keeping something secret and Gustav and I want to know what it is."

Erin opened the door of her car. "I was flying the plane in which your son arrived late today. This is your captain speaking . . ." She got in, closed the door, and giggled again.

She started her motor.

"Unbelievable . . . !" Mother whispered.

"Incredible!" He stood rooted to the spot in the midst of travelers as ecstatic as if they had been released from a nightmare, now streaming back to their cars, getting behind the wheel, distributing themselves onto the front and back seats. A tumultuous, endless chorus of honking began. Mother, who was very sensitive to noise, held her ears.

The Orthodox Jew and his wife skipped around on the asphalt like little children. As they danced, the man's sidelocks flew in all directions.

The chauffeur of the stretch limo got out of his enormous car for the first time. "I'm all by myself!" he called and opened all the doors to emphasize his point. The limousine was empty.

Six-fifteen. Gustav would still be able to reach his family before the beginning of Shabbat. Instead of feeling joyful, however, he felt unhappy: how could he leave the Tappan Zee before walking the rest of the length of the fatherbody, before he'd passed on from the solar plexus to the top of the head? He couldn't leave Father all alone!

He approached the Cadillac slowly, his head down, like a condemned man approaching the prison gate. Then suddenly turning around, he went up to Erin's car. She rolled down the window. "Get into your car. We're just about to get going," she whispered to him.

"May I call you sometime? Please, give me your telephone number. I find it so strange to have run into you here. Such a coincidence hardly ever happens. And why didn't you drive to Tarrytown along the east side of the Hudson? How did you stray onto this bridge?"

"I didn't stray at all. I've loved this bridge as far back as I can remember, all through my childhood and teens. In my mother's house, not far from here, in Sleepy Hollow, surrounded by fragrant bushes, clear streams, and tall trees, there's an attic room. From it you can see the tips of the steel uprights in the middle of the bridge. Except for sitting in the cockpit, there are few joys in my life to compare with crossing the Tappan Zee."

All around them, loud honking continued, even though no movement had reached the traffic at this end of the bridge yet.

He had to get to know this pilot better. He wanted to learn where the intimacy and energy came from he had sensed as soon as he saw her. He was standing just two feet from her and couldn't reach her. He was overcome by a feeling of powerlessness, sadness; he had the impression his life would slip away if he didn't act immediately.

There was a dazzling bolt of lightning over the west end of the bridge, followed instantaneously by a prolonged peal of thunder so powerful he couldn't hear Erin's answer.

She repeated her sentence, "We'll meet at the exit just beyond the end of the bridge and I'll take you to my mother's house."

A violent cloudburst came pouring down on the bridge. Gustav nodded. Erin rolled up her window. He dashed to the Cadillac, slaloming between bumpers as if on ice. He tore open the door of the car.

Mother was sitting on the passenger side, looking severe. "Now you're really going to catch cold. No undershirt and soaking wet from the rain. How can you be such an imbecile? . . . So? What did you arrange with her?"

"She's taking us home with her for a little while. We'll meet her at the exit off the bridge."

"What a marvelous woman! A pilot! Whoever heard of such a thing? People usually bore me to tears. Your father loved meeting people, but not me. That's why I usually talk so much, so I don't get too bored. At least if I can hear myself talk, then it's not so tedious! But I've never in my life met a woman pilot, have you? That such a thing should happen to your mother with her fear of flying! Later on, we'll tell her about those panic attacks I used to have. Think we should? I like having fears I've overcome; it even makes me proud. And we should let her know that I'm a member of an organization for the protection of people harmed by air traffic. Hopefully she'll be able to give me some advice on how we can improve our campaign against airplane noise in the future. Isn't it terribly cold for you in here? At least put on a sweater. She's such a great person, but how can she have the bad taste to buy herself a car like that? She must have tons of money, so why would she buy such a low-class heap?"

The rain drummed on the roof of their car, streamed down the windshield and the side windows.

"Poor Papa," sighed Rosa, "although the river water doesn't seem to bother him much either. On the contrary, maybe he's even enjoying it."

"I find her awfully attractive . . ."

"Who? Erin? You don't have to reveal everything that's going on inside your head to me, Burschi. You can keep some of it to yourself. But thanks for telling me. Anyway, I already noticed."

"I'm so smitten, I almost feel ill."

"That sounds awfully kitschy. I hope you're not going to tell her that in so many words. Now calm down. You'll see her again in just a little while. Besides, you're totally exhausted."

"It's true. I'm totally exhausted."

"Not ideal when you have to drive . . ."

"Not ideal . . ."

"Are you going to start repeating every word I say now?"

"I'm repeating every word you say now." Then after a pause, "I can't just leave Father lying here, pretend he isn't there, and drive on . . ."

"You can take a break. He won't disappear overnight. You can come back and visit him tomorrow, maybe bring the children along."

"On Shabbes? But we can't drive on Shabbat!"

"Then you'll just have to make an exception for your father. Or is God more important than your father?"

The line of cars had begun to move. Finally they could start, moving forward at a walking pace through rain that was coming down harder and harder. All around them, people were still honking in joyful relief. Gustav looked for Erin in his rear-view mirror. He'd lost sight of her. As a boy, he was tortured by a notion: nothing behind my back exists, and no one can prove otherwise. Because as soon as I turn around or look in a rearview mirror, it's back again. It manifests itself anew. Erin, however, remained invisible even when he turned around to look for her.

"Don't twist around like that when you're driving! What are you doing, anyway?" Mother scolded.

"It's so strange that my return ticket is gone . . ."

"What's so strange about it?"

"It's like a sign . . ."

"A sign? Of what?"

"That I should stay here."

"On the bridge?"

"No, in New York . . ."

"Nonsense. It's a sign there are criminals and scoundrels who break into cars, that's all."

"Why didn't they steal your money?"

"Because they got scared, the crooks. They saw us coming. It's childish to see it as a sign, Schatzi."

"Wouldn't it make you happy if I lived near you, and not so terribly far away anymore?"

"I really can't rack my brains about it right now. My brain is a cosmic goulash at the moment. Please don't make me even more *mevulveh* . . ." *Mevulveh*: one of Mother's favorite words, Yiddish for agitated, confused, a little crazy. There were also expressions only Mother seemed to know; *Gewittergoy* was one such word. It referred to men (never to women) whose appearance, manners, and speech were so utterly un-Jewish that if you came into contact with them, their boundless goyishness knocked your socks off.

"My God, I wish I had pizazz like your father used to," Mother groaned. "Then I wouldn't get so terribly tired." The pizazz guy, she often called him.

The mass of cars continued to move sluggishly forward. By now they had reached the dinosaur cage, and Gustav peered down through the rain onto the river far below. He felt a twinge in his solar plexus. The feeling of harboring moths and beetles in his stomach was getting stronger, until he finally knew what he had to do.

When they reached the place where they had earlier looked down onto Father's belly, he stopped the car and turned off the engine. Behind him, furious honking.

"For heaven's sake, what are you doing?"

"I'm staying here."

"Now that we're finally moving, you're stopping?"

From all directions, furious gazes were directed at him. He turned the ignition back on and maneuvered the Cadillac over to the right lane as if he were on a normal urban thoroughfare with parking spaces along the side. He stopped and opened his door.

Among the tumultuous sounds on the bridge and the murmur of the rain, the clatter of horse hooves was suddenly audible. At the same time, the rhythmic cry of a deep male voice was approaching. It was a man on a pitch-black stallion, riding along the empty opposite lane at a leisurely pace, beside the dividing barrier. Gustav could hear him but couldn't understand what he was saying.

"Close the door! It's horribly cold and the rain is blowing in," Mother begged.

He got out and slammed the door with exaggerated force. He leaned his back against the glass and metal. "I can't go on, Father," he whispered. "I can't take her anymore! How did you ever put up with her all those years, dear God! *Le mystère du couple* . . ."

Behind his back, she was knocking on the window. He didn't respond.

He watched the rider approach. Now he could hear his call more clearly. He repeated the same sentences over and over again like a mantra. He was warning them about the health risks of the toluene spill: "Danger! Toxic fumes ahead. Attention! Beware! Toxic fumes ahead. Danger: potential health hazard. The truck spilled toluene. Beware, toxic fumes ahead. Danger! Toluene affects the nervous system, causing tiredness, confusion, weakness, drunk-type actions, memory loss, nausea, loss of appetite, hearing and color vision loss. Toluene makes you feel light-headed, dizzy, and sleepy. Toluene can cause unconsciousness and even death." And then he started again, from the beginning: "Danger! Toxic fumes ahead. Attention! Toluene affects the nervous system . . ."

The rider, in blue jeans and with a soft face reminiscent of a flower child from the Sixties, passed close to Gustav at the same moment that Erin's Grand Am pulled up behind the Cadillac. ". . . potential for serious health problems. Beware, the truck spilled toluene . . ." They could still hear the rider calling. He trotted away, hooves clattering, toward the west end of the bridge.

The rain was letting up. Final streaks of lightning flickered across the sky and the thunder died away. The humidity formed a garment of mist that settled on Gustav's chest. It smelled of alder leaves and gasoline.

The pilot got out and came up to Gustav. "Why did you stop?"

"I—panicked."

"How come?"

"I couldn't see you in my rearview mirror anymore and I began to think I had only imagined meeting you. Someday when we know each other better, I'll tell you the other reason why I stopped."

"I'd like to know now."

"There's something I've still got to take care of here."

"Here? What do you mean, here?"

"On the bridge."

"I don't understand."

"May I explain it to you some other time?"

Mother was knocking on the window again.

"Would you mind if my mother rode with you and had a rest at your place? Write down the address and I'll follow in a little while."

"Will you promise to join us later?"

"I promise."

Erin returned to her car, wrote her address on a piece of paper, and even drew a little map so Gustav could find his way there after he exited at the eastern end of the bridge.

Mother had succeeded in turning the electrical system in the car back on. She opened one of the automatic windows. "So can you tell me what's going on now? And what that idiot on the horse is calling out all the time? You locked me in and I couldn't hear a word."

"Erin's going to take you to her house—to her mother's—and you can have a rest there. Whatever happens, I'm still staying on the bridge for a while."

"Please come with me. Don't stay here, really. Come on, don't be so crazy after all these hours of horror! Besides, you're all wet. You haven't even changed your clothes yet. Now that we can finally get going again, you want to—?! You can't be serious."

"When you get to Erin's house, you must call up Madeleine right away. Here's the number, on this piece of paper. Please don't lose it. Explain to her that I can't make it home this evening because I'm so exhausted . . . too exhausted to drive anymore. Even one more mile would be too much for me. Or tell her *you* won't let me drive anymore. I'm staying overnight in a hotel in Tarrytown, tell her that. I'm spending Shabbat there—"

"—which must not be broken, of course, not even under extraordinary circumstances—"

"And tomorrow evening, as soon as it's dark, as soon as three stars are visible in the sky, then I'll come, all rested and with my wits about me again. Madeleine will be furious, but she'll just have to accept it. What else can she do? Or she'll understand. Even that could happen!"

"Do you love her?"

"I think so."

"So you probably don't, because you can't answer such a question like that. If anybody asked your father, Do you love your wife? he would cry out with joy. And how, he'd say! She's the best! The most beautiful! I'd be lost without her! After forty-five years of marriage I'm just as much in love with my wife as when we first met! Her eyes, her sense of humor, her charm! And you? What's your answer? 'I think so.' Poor Em."

Erin waited patiently while mother and son ended their conversation.

Rosa got out of the car and looked at her child with desperate uncertainty and boundless incomprehension. "Don't be angry that I'm leaving you by yourself, Burscherle. I'm sorry." She walked toward the pilot, turned toward him once more. "I'm sure you'll miss me someday even more than you miss your father. At least put on a sweater! And there's one more thing I have to tell you. It's been running through my head all day long, ever since I picked you up. In the past, any time I caught sight of you, there was something in the air, something that touched me, as if the Messiah had come through the door. And when you went away again—Father could feel it, too—whenever you left the room, then it was as if the Messiah was leaving us. It felt like you had us under a spell. But that's all gone now, completely gone. I don't know since when. You've . . . lost your aura."

Erin opened the passenger-side door from inside the car. The sight of her stretching her torso over to reach the door handle! How Gustav yearned for her body, the warmth of her limbs, for her laugh, the curve of her lips.

She turned on her engine, cranked down the window, rolled past him at a crawl. She handed him the piece of paper with her address and whispered, "Hurry up! You promised me!"

And what if Erin weren't an American Airlines pilot? Maybe she's a swindler, a burglar, the one who stole my stuff. Perhaps even now she's driving Rosa to the lair she shares with her heinous accomplices, where Mother will be robbed, tortured, murdered. They'll saw up her body and throw her limbs into the Hudson for the fish to eat.

He waved feebly at the two of them.

They waved back.

And drove away.

He immediately felt as if he'd been freed from an iron yoke. Mother stole all his strength, like a vampire, just as Father—while he was still healthy—had sucked out all his strength. Ludwig often said to him when they parted, "I'm amazed at your patience with the two of us, my Burscherle. If I'd had parents like us, I certainly wouldn't have been as patient with them . . ."

Alone. Alone at last. How different your whole body feels, from head to toe, as soon as you're alone. Not with your own children, not with your mother, not with your wife, not with friends.

Completely alone with yourself and the fatherbody.

Here I am, my father, he called down. We're alone at last.

16

It smelled damp, cool, and fresh. Iron-gray fog settled onto the bridge.

He stood at the railing. Never before in his life had he felt so burned out, so utterly weak, so pale as he did on this Friday afternoon, the sixth of August, 1999.

For a few seconds—a few minutes?—he fell asleep on his feet.

Here I am, my father, alone at last. I'm so tired, Father. How you lie there, stretched out from pier to pier! It's impressive, like every exaggeration. My river-god father. Warm hands and a hot heart? Where were we? How fast you could type on your

big, black, heavy typewriter, which you gave me on my ninth
birthday. But then you couldn't survive without it, couldn't
write anymore. I seldom have seen you so unhappy, so bash-
ful as you were on my tenth birthday, when you asked me
to return your present from the previous year, the beloved
Underwood you picked up for a carton of cigarettes in 1945,
in the ruins of Berlin, where you found yourself shortly after
Germany's collapse, a liberator in the guise of a reporter for
the *Los Angeles Times*.

You're turning your snow-white back to me. No one was
permitted to turn his back to you. Whenever that happened,
you became apoplectic. You never could stand it when people
didn't give you their absolute, full attention. Mother and I, all
your friends (although basically, you had hardly any friends;
you had no time to cultivate friendships), people you didn't
know—we all had to look you in the eye whenever we were
sitting with you. Just don't ever turn our backs to you! That
outraged you more than any other sin one could have committed. Your quick temper knew no bounds, and as a sign of
your disgust with us, you would hold your flat hand up to your
forehead like the bill of a cap. I think you overreacted so much
when someone turned their back to you because you were,
surprisingly, superstitious. Turning one's back triggered something in you that had to do with the spirit world. If a black cat
ran across your path, you would immediately come to a halt,
bend down to whatever country road, city street, or forest path
you were on, pick up some earth or stones, and throw them
in a great arc over your shoulder—every single time, without
exception. And if the cat wasn't black and didn't cross your

path from left to right, but rather at an angle or from right to left, you would stop anyway and exorcise its dark powers. For safety's sake, you said, you never know. You would pick up dirt or whatever was on the ground and throw it over your shoulder. You, the scientist, the rational thinker. If you accidentally spilled some salt, you would pick up the crystals and throw them behind you—to ward off trouble. And if you were feeling particularly good, both healthy and successful, then you would immediately knock on wood and murmur: Just don't flaunt it! The number thirteen, however, was your lucky number, not an unlucky one. You declared the thirteenth of every month a day of celebration. You considered Fridays that fell on the thirteenth especially auspicious days. Superstition was your constant companion. You forbade me ever to walk beneath scaffolding. As soon as we came to a building under repair or renovation, we'd cross to the other side of the street. To walk beneath scaffolding meant tempting fate unnecessarily.

But you were allowed to tempt fate. You tried to do harm to people who had done harm to you. The president of an elite New England university offered you a chair in nuclear physics and you enthusiastically accepted. When it came time to sign the contract, however, it turned out that the job had previously been promised to another colleague who was to begin teaching the next month. Whereupon you cursed the university president—and exactly one year later, Professor Sinclair Jacobs happened to be visiting the Macedonian city of Skopje just when it was destroyed by a devastating earthquake. He died under the rubble of his hotel.

Gustav surrendered himself to the illusion that he suddenly had wings, wings stretching out for yards. He felt them to be not a gift from heaven, however, but a burden. They made his weary body even heavier and more cumbersome. His feet were made of lead. His shoes seemed so bulky they felt like tractor tires.

He inched forward, pushed along by his heavy wings, until he came to the spot he had been yearning to reach for several hours: Father's third nipple. In keeping with the monstrous Goliath body lying far below the bridge, the nipple was as large as a trophy, the kind tennis players are awarded. My Father, he called through the drifting fog, I am your wisp of fog! How many boys in this world can say with such confidence: *I am your son!*

The wiry, grayish white hair on Father's chest was sparse, but much less so than on his own, where only a few little hairs sprouted. He pulled at them, enjoying a few seconds of pain.

He was thirsty and hungry, light-headed, as on Yom Kippur.

Father, I can hardly stay on my feet. I want to come to you, lie down next to you. I am so frightfully weary.

How frightfully weary Father had been when Gustav paid him a surprise visit in his hotel room in Hamburg, five weeks before Ludwig's stroke. Gustav had an appointment with the director of a bank who was not satisfied with the mink coat she had had made to order in Vienna. Richard Lichtmann asked his partner to reassure the young woman, the heiress of a private bank, and deliver their promise to her in person that a new coat was being prepared. By chance, Father was also in Hamburg on the same day, the guest of honor at the conference "Opportunities for New Forms of Energy." Gustav arrived at the airport at nine-thirty in the morning and took a cab to the Hotel Vier Jahreszeiten, which happened to be next to the bank where he had an appointment with the banker late in the afternoon. He knew Father's room number, slipped past the reception desk, and knocked on the door of Room 423. No answer. He knocked louder. Four times. Five times. Finally Father opened the door. He was stark naked and covered from head to toe with quickly dissolving patches of foam that left a moist trail on the soft carpeting. He hurried back into the warm tub. To Gustav, Ludwig's body seemed especially short and thin on that morning in the hotel; he looked like a frog, a small, naked frog. My little frogfather. Ludwig sank back into the water and closed his eyes. He had slept badly. Much too much light had penetrated through slits in the drapes. The blankets were too heavy for him, the pillows too skimpy. He looked the same as he did when he was suffering from facial paralysis. Twenty years had gone by since then. Overnight, his features had become immobile. He was in terrible pain, but the doctors couldn't discover what was causing the condition and feared it might be a brain tumor. They ordered tests, but the results were inconclusive. The only place where his torments were bearable was in the bathtub. For hours and days he lay in the hot water, slept there, read his mail, leafed through scientific studies, ran more hot water. After a week of this, a friend who had emigrated to California, the native Berliner and famous dentist to the Hollywood stars, Friedrich Silber, was passing through Vienna and paid him a visit. Silber immediately diagnosed the cause of Ludwig's condition: rotten teeth with suppurating roots. Father hadn't been to a dentist in years. Only after weeks of complicated treatments did the facial paralysis disappear.

For the first time since then, on that morning in Room 423 of the Hotel Vier Jahreszeiten in Hamburg, the son discerned in his father's face signs of old age. He sat next to him, on the toilet seat cover, balancing a tray on his knees and eating and drinking the remains of Father's breakfast. On this morning, Ludwig talked about money, something he had never done before. But on this morning, he mentioned his savings, his reserve funds. He was certainly influenced by the fact that his son had an appointment with a banker. "The money I have in the account in Berlin is to provide for my old age. As you know, it is my categorical wish—and I will do everything within my power to fulfill it—to live to be a hundred and twenty. You don't die of old age, you die of illness, and I don't intend to fall ill any time soon!"

Gustav kept on walking farther east.

Once it had become clear that the blockage would not be cleared any time soon, the bridge had been closed to all further traffic at its western end. Now the traffic jam had ended but the closure remained in effect, and Gustav was all alone on the Tappan Zee. The entire length of the bridge was as if swept clean—except for his rental car, the stationmaster's abandoned motor home, and extravagant piles of trash: plastic bottles, aluminum cans, lost items of clothing, basketballs, paper. He was the only survivor: no other human, no animal remained. The earth had not been destroyed, but all life was extinguished. Was this the auto-free paradise Father had once dreamed of in his pamphlet against the flood of cars?

For the first time, vapors from the toluene spill reached his nose. He had the taste of fingernail polish, wood varnish, beauty salon in his mouth. These vapors neither irritated his mucous membranes and eyes nor caused any nausea. His slight dizziness, however, might have had some connection to them. Gustav should have turned around on the spot and gone back to his car, but instead he stayed where he was, hanging over the railing and looking down at Father's shoulders, neck, and clavicle.

A police siren approached from the western side. The howling patrol car stopped next to the Cadillac. Right behind it, two tow trucks pulled up. One positioned itself directly in front of the Cadillac, the other next to the stationmaster's motor home. Gustav felt too weak to make it back to his rental car; at a jog it wouldn't have taken him much more than three minutes. He was too exhausted to fight for the car and its contents. He couldn't handle being issued a ticket for lack of proper identification, couldn't stand having to put his signature on documents. In fact, he preferred to let the Cadillac—together with the suitcases, his jacket, and his carry-on luggage—disappear.

From his distant vantage point, he watched the front of the rental car being lifted up by the tow truck's crane, as if they were hanging his—Gustav's—mortal frame on a meat hook. He had an impulse to tear open his mouth and hurl a primal scream into the heavens, but remained motionless and silent.

Then the two trucks set off with their quarry in tow, coming in his direction, led by the patrol car. He feared the convoy would stop and he would be questioned. What's a lone pedestrian doing on the Tappan Zee? Would he by any chance be the owner of the Cadillac? Where can I go? thought Gustav. I've got to hide!

Meanwhile, Rosa Rubin had arrived at Erin's mother's house.
Josephine Tassel was one of those people who enjoy unex-
pected company. That alone made her as drastically different
from Gustav's mother "as a flamingo is from a crocodile," as Rosa
said to Erin. The mansion, surrounded by a parklike garden, was
one of the most paradisiacal estates Mother had ever seen. Mrs.
Tassel, only heiress of a shoe manufacturer, had grown up in
Sleepy Hollow, in the same house she still occupied. She hardly
traveled at all, she declared, had never been to Europe or Asia
or Africa. Not just from fear of flying, she laughed. No, really
not, and besides, as Erin's mother she could fly for a fraction of
the usual price. No, it was because she was so devoted to her
house and garden and her four cats. Erin's mother divulged this
information only a few minutes after her daughter had told her
how and where she had met Mrs. Rubin and Rosa had visited
the dancehall-sized bathroom and washed her hands, neck, and
face with violet-blue hand soap. Rosa then asked to use the telephone. She had to call her daughter-in-law, she said, and in-
form her about the events of the last few hours.

After Rosa had ticked off the messages Gustav had assigned
her to deliver, Madeleine at first remained completely silent.
Then after a while, she began to whimper softly. Mother didn't
try to comfort her or calm her down. She just said, "All this is
just as hard for him as it is for you." Then Madeleine began to
scream so loudly that Erin and Mrs. Tassel, standing in the next
room, could hear the shrill voice from the receiver, which Rosa
was holding some distance from her ear. She'd had just about
enough of this family, Madeleine shouted. She accused Rosa
of persuading Gustav to leave the car in Tarrytown this evening

just because she wanted to spend one more night alone with her son. Where was he now, she wanted to know. Why wasn't he at the hotel with Rosa yet? Why didn't she put him on the line? Something funny was going on. Rosa was lying to her. She insisted on speaking to Gustav before Shabbat began, barely two hours from now. And who had driven Rosa to Tarrytown? She couldn't take it anymore. She wouldn't keep playing along. This was the end.

Mother felt so worn out afterward that she asked Mrs. Tassel if she could lie down for a moment. They led her up to the third floor, to a guest room next to the nursery where Erin had slept as a child. From the windows of this tiny room, furnished like a doll house, one could see the peaks of the Tappan Zee, just as Erin had described them. Rosa was happy to see the bridge again. She immediately felt connected to Gustav. Mrs. Tassel brought her a glass of orange juice and chocolate cookies, said she was going to prepare a light supper for Rosa and her son—who would certainly arrive by then—and closed the door of the guest room.

Rosa felt as if she were floating on a cloud, even though Madeleine's furious outburst had hurt her and made her uneasy. She took off her shoes, immediately fell back onto the quilt that covered the soft yet firm double bed, swung her legs up as well, and in less than a minute was fast asleep. Not even the launch of a Saturn V rocket from Josephine Tassel's garden could have woken her.

17

Gustav turned his back to the roadway and pressed against the railing, trying to make himself invisible. The police convoy roared past without noticing him. He didn't look around, didn't get a look at the Cadillac even out of the corner of his eye, and he remained like that until all sound had died away on the wet road surface.

Alone again with the empty bridge.

I'm very hungry, Father, he whispered. My head is spinning. I'm holding tight to the railing. I have no choice; I must climb down to you. Gustav knew he was unlikely to succeed in this descent, that it was extremely dangerous. Even in the best physical and mental condition, he wouldn't be able to safely overcome the obstacles that were to be expected. He couldn't climb down to the level of the bridge foundation without placing himself in mortal danger.

He clambered onto the edge of the bridge—a gust of wind forced him back onto the road. He tried again, stood on the railing holding tight to a lamppost; stood there, looking out over the gigantic surface of the Hudson. The wind swallowed the noise of the river. During a momentary lull, the distant barking of a dog could be heard, then it blew past him. He knelt down, looked for a handhold—an iron bar or a strut that would allow him to seek a new foothold. Or was his only possibility to jump?

He took a deep breath.

Knelt down on the railing.

He hitched himself dangerously far out over the edge of the bridge and let his left foot dangle, seeking a foothold, finding only emptiness, depth. I'm coming to you, Father, he whispered, even if it costs me my life. Your life is my life. My life is your life. Who am I? What have I done with my life? I should have listened to you back then, when Lichtmann offered to make me his partner. I should never have paid attention to Mother's advice. I would have been one of the most important historians of our time. There aren't many experts on the Hundred Years War, Father. Surprisingly, not more than four or five outstanding names. I could have gone far.

I'm very hungry, Father. I haven't eaten anything since the midday snack on the plane, eight hours ago. Not a nut, not a breadcrumb, not a raisin. Mother ate up everything I bought at the gas station. She offered me a handful of nuts, but I wasn't hungry yet. I'm really thirsty, Father, haven't had a drop to drink for hours.

With the toe of his left shoe he was able to find a hold on a narrow ledge beneath and a little set back from the railing. With his long legs spread wide apart, he lifted the right one, pulled it clumsily over the railing, clung tight with numb hands, now lowered his right foot to the ledge as well, and slid his belly over the edge. Not even when rock climbing in the mountains high above Tarasp, his favorite spot, had he moved so cautiously and at the same time so clumsily and fearfully. His left foot now groped fifteen or twenty inches below the narrow ledge for a new hold. And couldn't find one. And then was able to after all. He found a hold for his right foot as well and felt as if his fingertips were so far from the tips of his toes that his body must have doubled in length. He let go with one hand. It took all his strength to press his thighs, belly, chest, and one arm against the metal railing. He made another attempt to climb farther down, and a third, and a fourth. Now he was swaying between the projecting concrete ledge and the surface of the water, dangling high above Father's head.

The back of Ludwig's head lay in the water, his face turned toward the huge steel struts of the pylons. Are your eyes open? Are they closed? Gustav hung on tight, painfully twisting his neck, farther and farther around, and looked down onto Father's closed eyelids, the size of the round teak dining table of his childhood.

Suddenly, his left foot slipped and was hanging over the abyss. In a flash, everything began to slide, but a fraction of a second later Gustav was able to clutch back onto the iron struts, a little more firmly than before.

He dangled between heaven and Hudson. His shirt hung in tatters on his back.

If he had been completely out of shape, if he hadn't trained his arm muscles for years with ludicrous-looking weights, then he would surely have plunged into the river. His heart was pounding like a jackhammer. He couldn't get enough air, and remained motionless for a long time, surprised that he hadn't lost consciousness. He could picture Rosa's call to Madeleine, perhaps in the middle of the night, or by tomorrow morning at the latest. It would take forever for Madeleine to pick up the receiver—on Shabbat the Orthodox answer the telephone only in extreme emergencies. He could hear Madeleine's tirade against her mother-in-law. She would hold Rosa solely responsible for the catastrophe. He could picture Madeleine's collapse and then her drive to the bridge, in a taxi, even on the sacred day. Once again, her life would be reaching a culmination point in re-current, all-too-familiar pain. Surely that's how she would feel. When she was nine years old, her father had left her mother. He'd fallen in love with his older brother's stepdaughter. His parents had been deported from France just like Rosa's par-ents. He too had felt abandoned his entire life. But he simply repeated what had been done to him. He left his only daugh-ter, saw her only occasionally after that, on the High Holy Days, and would greet her with the same words every time: You see, my angel, the weather is always gorgeous on the High Holy Days. Mark my words, no matter where you hap-pen to be, you'll always find a cloudless blue sky on Rosh

Hashanah, Yom Kippur, on Sukkoth and Simchas Torah, want to bet?

Gustav now hazarded a continuation of his descent, observing himself the way you observe a stranger doing a magic trick. Cautiously, rung by rung, he struggled down the giant bridge pylon toward the water. The fog had dispersed. You could see a great distance through the clear, clean air. Despite his perilous situation, he was able to make out the distant skyline of Manhattan. And he yearned for New York as never before, felt that this city of majestic bridges was his true home. At that very moment, he decided that if he survived this day, this evening, this night, he would move to New York for good.

An hour had passed since he began his descent. He paused frequently and when he did, he held fast to the iron struts of the pylon. The closer he got to the surface of the water, the more outrageous his adventure seemed. The fatherhead was big as a tethered hot-air balloon; it lay still on the foundation of the bridge pylon, only now and then rocking almost imperceptibly to the rhythm of the waves that sometimes washed over the body.

It was a miracle that Gustav had managed to climb down to the river without falling and without injuring himself. If guardian angels in fact exist, then at least one of them had been his constant companion over the course of the last hour. His head ached with a deeper, more gnawing pain than ever before. Hunger and exhaustion joined forces balefully, but his

pride at the successful descent helped him put up with the almost unbearable throbbing.

Twilight began to fall. It was the moment when Shabbat began, the high point of creation. Scholars ask, Why is Shabbat
the high point of creation? And they answer, Because it was
the first moment of rest, the first day God paused, kept still.

Gustav found himself near the east bank, could see the
rails of the New York-to-Albany line clearly, hear the clatter
of the trains and the wail of their whistles.

He jumped the final six feet down to the huge foundation, spraining his left ankle—he hardly noticed the pain. The
great breakwater of the pier seemed to him like a raft rocking
in the sea. He picked up one of the numerous empty tin cans—
the tattered label read "Peeled Tomatoes"—and threw it as far
as he could. He now stood right next to his father's head, which
reached up higher than his navel. Gustav touched the thick
shock of white hair on Ludwig Rubin's head. It didn't feel silky;
it felt more like hemp. Gustav's whole body was trembling.
He still hesitated to touch the skin of Father's face. The smell
of plants impossible to grow in the climate of North America
reached his nostrils, a smell he knew from Israel, from the villa
of an Armenian customer of Lichtmann & Rubin, Furriers, to
whom he had personally delivered a sable coat in Jerusalem
several years ago. During Gustav's sojourn in her house, the
woman spoke of nothing but her father, who had died three
months earlier and whom she had loved much more than her
children or husband, as she declared in a cheerful voice. The
memory of the odor in this customer's house—a combination

of myrrh and juniper—overlay the smell under the bridge, which emanated from motor oil, dead batteries, algae, and the tin cans that had collected there.

But then Gustav felt for Father's face after all, for a spot above the bushy, bristly hairs of his left eyebrow, on his forehead, near the hairline. Heard Mother's words ringing in his ears: your father has an unbelievably hard head. He butts it right through any wall in his way. Whatever notion he gets into his head, he makes it happen.

The son felt the tough elephant skin, ran his hand over creases, moles, and uneven patches, the large nose, the thick lips. Ludwig's mother had warned Rosa on their wedding day: when my son gets a fat lower lip, then he's overdone things. It means he's overtired. Here, on his breakwater bed, his lower lip was thicker than it had ever been in his life. And he had pulled his upper lip downward, as he always did when he looked in the mirror, for as long as Gustav could remember. No sooner did Ludwig look in a mirror than he pulled down his lip. It was a reflex he couldn't control. Just one time, Father, try it just once in your life, Gustav had begged for decades. Try not to make that face when you look in a mirror! He couldn't do it. He never succeeded.

He didn't dare touch the ear, big as a living room rug. With this ear Father had listened to Led Zeppelin through a set of headphones that weighed at least a pound, lying on Gustav's bed in the little hotel room where his son had slept in the late Sixties, next door to his parents' room in Berlin Grunewald.

They had lived in that hotel for months. Father had accepted a guest professorship at the Technical University, and for its duration Gustav attended school in Berlin, smoked hashish in the afternoons and at night, and completely abandoned himself to rock music. Only Ludwig was privy to his son's drug-induced fantasies. Only he knew about the double life of the adolescent who hardly slept anymore, got stoned, and listened to his records until the wee hours. Father wanted to hear what Gustav was listening to. At 33⅓ rpm on the Dual turntable, his son played him the first track on the Led Zeppelin II album, "Whole Lotta Love," Gustav's favorite song of all time. Ludwig arose from his son's narrow bed with the words "You've opened up a whole new world for me."

Gustav placed both his hands on the closed eyelid of Father's left eye. The skin felt softer here, like silk or velvet. Did the lid tremble? Father's head, which seemed to know everything that human intelligence was capable of knowing at the end of the twentieth century. One could ask him any question and he always had an answer that would carry the questioner further, persuade him of something, open new horizons, and reveal overlappings and interconnections. "I'm a high-spirited pessimist, an encourager, a collector of rays of hope." That's how Ludwig described himself, and everyone who met him experienced him as such. Did he have any enemies at all?

Gustav touched Father's furrowed brow. Did the deep lines resemble certain letters? They ran not just horizontally, but vertically as well. Were they Hebrew letters? Shin, aleph, mem? He took the little camera out of his pants pocket and snapped a picture of the forehead. And covered it with kisses, again and again. He felt ashamed as his fingertips brushed across it, a regret that more than a quarter century had hardly diminished. It was all my fault, Father! It only happened because of me. I've never asked your forgiveness, he whispered.

The arrival of Richard Nixon and Secretary of State Henry Kissinger in Salzburg in the summer of 1973 had been anticipated. It was to be a two-day stop on their way to a summit in Moscow. At the Salzburg airport, where Air Force One was supposed to land early in the evening, thousands had gathered to protest the Vietnam War. At the time, Gustav's heart defect had not been operated on yet, and Rosa was afraid he would overexert himself at the demonstration if someone didn't look after him. She sent Ludwig from Vienna to Salzburg to be with their son. It took Father a long time to find Gustav in the crowd of young people smoking marijuana and waving protest signs. Then they waited for hours in the hayfields surrounding the landing strip, chanting Ho-Ho-Ho Chi Minh! Ho-Ho-Ho Chi Minh! in chorus, again and again, singing the Internationale, and shouting, Create two, three, many Vietnams! Destroy what's destroying you! Get stoned, be free, a little terror if it has to be! At twilight, the counterforce assembled on the opposite side of the runway: two hundred policemen in gray greatcoats, armed with truncheons and Plexiglas shields. Through megaphones they ordered the demonstrators to disperse immediately; the president's plane was due to land shortly. A cry of elation rose from the crowd; they started occupying the runway. Searchlights were trained on the war protesters and without a second warning, the men in uniform stormed the landing strip of the Salzburg Airport. They drew their truncheons and wielded them like fur hunters clubbing baby seals and their mothers on the

Newfoundland ice for the pelts that Gustav would begin selling just a few years later. He started to run without once turning back to look for his sixty-year-old father. He ran as fast as his racing heart would allow until he had escaped the policemen and felt safe again. Ludwig, however, had been clubbed to the ground and beaten about the head and back. Although almost completely out of breath, he had cried out, "I am Ludwig Rubin! Don't you recognize me?" But it didn't do him any good. They only laughed, the men in uniform. And then Air Force One landed and an official black limousine conveyed Nixon and Kissinger to Klessheim Palace, where they spent the night.

That same evening, a friend of Father's from London was visiting the Rubins, Lord Kennet, a Labour member of the House of Lords and a Harvard classmate of Henry Kissinger. For years, he had been singing Kissinger's praises to Ludwig. Although the Englishman didn't agree with Kissinger's politics, he admired his intelligence and sparkling wit. Lord Kennet and Father wanted to call Kissinger up as soon as he arrived in Salzburg and arrange for the three men to meet at noon the next day. While Gustav and Father, who had sustained a wound on his forehead, were on their way to the emergency room in a taxi (a doctor they had called over declared the wound "an unspectacular head injury" so the ambulance had refused to take Ludwig), Lord Kennet, who as yet knew nothing about the demonstration because back then the Rubins had no television in their apartment in Vienna, called up Klessheim Palace to welcome his friend Henry to Europe. The White House switchboard, installed in Salzburg for the duration of Nixon's visit to Austria, had answered. Lord Kennet pronounced the code word and was immediately put through to his friend Henry. Since he had hardly any commitments in Salzburg anyway, Kissinger was looking forward to a reunion with his old university friend. Lord Kennet's suggestion that he bring the famous nuclear physicist Ludwig Rubin to lunch with him, however, was angrily rejected by Kissinger. An Austrian television camera had caught the moment when Father was being beaten— his outcry and the jeers of the police. One could even make out the lobster-red welts rising on his forehead. It had all been on the evening news. While Ludwig, struck by clubs on his forehead and back, was pulling out his passport, you could hear in the background the noise of planes landing, full of advance security personnel. It was Rosa who, despite all that, had made the arrangements for the meeting of Kennet and Kissinger at noon on the following day. It actually took place: Mother chose a restaurant for the two of them, the Fondachhof in the Parsch neighborhood of Salzburg. It was she who called from Vienna to order a table, without revealing who the two "difficult guests" were for whom she was reserving the most beautiful, quietest table outside in the garden. The bruises on Father's forehead, expertly bandaged in the Salzburg emergency room and slowly receding thanks to numerous medications, remained visible for weeks after the incident. Father, my dear, poor dad, Gustav murmured, allow me to ask your forgiveness here and now. I ought to have been at your side, protecting you. Perhaps I would have succeeded in preserving you from the police truncheons.

Gustav's shoe got stuck in the mud. His injured ankle began to hurt after all. He lost his balance, sank to his knees, lay in the mud. He struggled to his feet again. Everything was wet and muddy: his pants, torn shirt, shoes. He took off his shoes, sought to steady himself on the metal grid of the breakwater. I'm floating on the surface of the caisson, he whispered to himself. I'm lying on one of the foundations of the Tappan Zee. The caissons are the fathers and mothers of every bridge construction. Without caissons, no large bridge would exist on earth.

He hung onto the sparse, whitish gray hairs on the back of his father's head. They felt like mooring ropes.

Gustav tipped sideways, reached out his legs, let himself slide around the dome of Father's head, lay stretched out next to his skull, clinging to the fatherhair, pressing his wet, half-naked torso against the back of Ludwig's head, clutching it tightly as Ludwig had clutched Rosa tightly his entire married life—at night, early in the morning, in the hour of the wolf, in the marriage bed. He heard a soft jangling in his ears: "It is enough; now, O Lord, take away my life; for I am not better than my fathers."

A curtain of darkness settled onto the Hudson. The first stars appeared. Lying pressed against the fatherhead, Gustav whispered the Shema—Hear, O Israel!—and the Eighteen Benedictions, which one must always speak standing up. Barely audible, he sang the song that greets the bride, Likrat Kallah. Shabbat is the bride you take into your heart for a day.

And forgetting all about his overpowering hunger, his unquenchable thirst, he fell asleep.

18

He was awakened by a low putt-putting.

It came closer, got louder, drew closer and closer. He held tight to the fatherskull, turned his head, and saw the outline of a small motorboat in the darkness, gliding through the waves of the Hudson. Mother had sent them out to look for him, and now they had found him. At last he was saved. I don't want to be saved, Father. I don't want to turn around and go back. Help me, Father. Please help me as you always did. You always gave me advice, lying in the steaming bathtub while I sat beside you. Tell me, how can I shed my skin, leave the story of my life behind? I don't want to go on living as I have up to now. Should I devote myself to my studies again—my research, my passion, history—as you recommended back when I'd stopped listening to you and took only Mother's advice?

A small light was attached to the bow of the boat, like the phosphorescent night-light the size of his hand that had illuminated the nights of his childhood, bathing his room in feeble green light and calming his fear before he fell asleep. Until he was thirteen or fourteen he had to have that light with him at all times, took it along on trips as well: in hotels, when his parents went out, in foreign cities. How difficult it often was to scare up that same wan, electric green if they had forgotten to bring it along or when the foreign outlets didn't match its plug.

"Gustav?" What a soft, beautiful voice. "Gustav Rubin . . . !" The voice of a policewoman? A firewoman? So friendly, so mild? The putt-putting stopped. The boat drifted closer to him. The figure rose and threw him a line. He caught it even though he was still lying down.

Erin, it was Erin. Her hair wasn't in a braid anymore; now it framed her lovely face like a lion's mane, falling to her shoulders in thick, reddish cascades. She jumped out onto the top of the breakwater. She was wearing sturdy shoes with good soles that kept her from slipping on the wet metal. She tied up the boat.

"I was looking for you a long time, then it suddenly occurred to me—it was some sort of inspiration—that you might be down here. Your mother is very worried about you. She insisted on coming along with me, but I was able to dissuade her. She thinks you jumped into the water. Or fell in while taking pictures . . . We've got to let her know that I've found you. You must be very hungry . . ." She had brought food for him. "Here, have some!"

Didn't Erin see Father's body? How could she stay so calm in the face of the titanic sight of him?

"Let's not call her right away!" he requested. "Let's be . . . alone, at least for a few minutes . . ."

"First you must have something to eat and drink. And then you can stand up. You've still got a long way to go . . ."

It felt so good to hear her voice. It was as though she were giving him a kiss.

"Have you noticed, there's a wonderful odor of juniper and myrrh?" he asked her.

"You've got to put your mother's mind at ease."

"I can't talk to her now. I want to be just with you, hidden from the whole world."

"Mom? Please tell Mrs. Rubin that I've fou—— . . . Yes, Mrs. Rubin. I've found him . . . No, I think he doesn't want to talk to you right now."

He could clearly hear Mother's tone of command: "Give him to me immediately! What do you mean he doesn't want to talk to me? Please stay out of our family affairs. He's my child!" Erin held out the cell phone in the direction of the fatherear, holding it out to Gustav.

"Turn it off, quick!" he whispered. He got up very slowly, as if wrapped in heavy dream clothes. The pain in his ankle was torture, like being pierced by nails.

Erin stepped toward Gustav. He embraced her as vehemently as if he were in full possession of his strength.

"My father would have liked you enormously . . ."

She gently disengaged herself. He took the little phone she was still holding and that was still connected to his mother and threw it as far out into the Hudson as he could.

Erin hit at him with both fists. "You're crazy. You're a lunatic. I wish I'd never met you and your mother!" She tore her hair.

He tried to embrace her again, without success.

"That was—my umbilical cord to the world, Gustav."

"Forgive me. It was the umbilical cord to my world, too."

It took her a while to calm down. "Now eat something. I brought it for you," she said. "My mother always gives me a basket like this when I leave the house on an overseas flight."

He sat down cross-legged next to the fatherbrow. She still couldn't see the gigantic head! Later in the night, when she lay next to him, pressed against him, he would ask her if she had seen it or not.

She sat down next to Gustav and handed him his food.

He spoke the Kiddush, the blessing of the wine: Blessed art thou, our Lord God, Lord of the world, who hath created the fruit of the vine. While Gustav greeted the Shabbat in Hebrew, Erin listened, felt ill at ease, as she always did when visiting a foreign house of worship. Praise be to you, our Lord God, Lord of the world, who sanctifies us through His commandments and allows us to partake of the sacred rest of Shabbat, in love and cordiality, in memory of the work of creation. And he spoke a blessing over the bread Erin had brought in the basket, which he broke and sprinkled with salt. He handed a piece to Erin just as he handed them to Madeleine and the children on Friday evenings. And then he bit into the chicken—unkosher, because the animal had not been slaughtered and allowed to bleed according to ritual. He ate and drank in eager bites and swallows, like a man rescued after days and nights wandering in the desert. It was the first time in years, since his turn to the religious path, that he was eating food that didn't conform to the Law. Even in mortal danger, the great rabbis of history chose to starve to death rather than sin by taking even one bite of meat that wasn't kosher.

"Where's your car?!" Erin seemed worried. "I can't see it anywhere . . ."

He put a finger to his lips.

The Chimney Rock red came from Northern California, a soft, round 1994 cabernet sauvignon. Wine must be kosher too. It must come from barrels that with absolute certainty have never been used for ecclesiastical communion wine. It is supposed to come only from dedicated barrels for kosher wine, otherwise one mustn't touch it. It was the first time in years he had drunk unkosher wine.

Erin took a swallow from his cup. They could see the gleam of isolated lights on shore. The bridge lights had been turned on, and weak reflections reached them here.

"My parents met in New York harbor," Gustav suddenly began, "not far from here, maybe thirty miles away . . . fifty-one years ago, in the middle of the summer of 1948. Father had gone aboard the ship *Liberté* with a friend bound for Calais and was sitting with him in his cabin until the liner was ready to sail. At the last minute, a young Viennese woman showed up to say good-bye to the friend. She had only a fleeting acquaintance with him, had known him only a few weeks, but liked him a lot and had the intention of becoming his girlfriend. She was sad that he was returning to Europe without her. In the cabin of that ocean liner, she saw my father for the first time. When the ship's horn sounded, they bid good-bye to their mutual friend and had to disembark quickly. Then, in the twilight, they went for a little walk together along the docks. Two months later, they were married . . ."

Erin remained silent. She seemed to Gustav very different from earlier, in the downpour. He often had this impression when he ran into someone again whom he had first met in the company of others and now encountered alone. In such cases, he was often surprised, disappointed, embarrassed.

She stroked his hand. "It's time you said good-bye . . . to the bridge," she said. "I promised your mother I'd bring you back to her."

"I'm going to stay with my father tonight . . ."

Erin didn't know what he meant. Was there such a thing as the Father, the Son, and the Holy Ghost in Judaism? She didn't dare ask.

". . . and besides, I'm not allowed to drive on Shabbat," he continued. "You're not allowed to leave the place where you happen to be at the beginning of Shabbat even to walk or drive to a place nearby. So even on foot, I wouldn't be allowed to go more than two thousand cubits—that's less than a mile— from this location until tomorrow evening."

"Didn't you just eat something you weren't supposed to eat?"

He devoured everything Erin had brought him. They drained the bottle of wine to the dregs.

He was cold. They were both cold. And then he sank down again, pressed tight again against the fatherhead, as before, and turned his head toward Erin. "Come and snuggle up to me. I'm cold. Come up close to me."

"You've got to go back to your mother. You've got to go back to your wife, back to your children, your life."

"I shall stay here with my father. He needs me. Can you be with me tonight? When do you have to leave again?"

"In three days . . . I'm flying to Sydney."

"You weren't at all afraid when the engine failed! Your voice sounded so confident and unconcerned." He envied her. When she made the announcement, the thought that ran through his head was, only a Gentile can be so fearless.

"I'm always afraid when I fly," she replied. "As a child, I refused to board any airplanes at all. Our visits to relatives in Florida always took forever. The first time I flew, I was sixteen. The stewardess asked me if I wanted to see the cockpit. She saw me trembling and thought it would help if I could be in the cockpit. That was an amazing moment, gazing down on the world from up in the sky, flying from New York to Miami. Controlling the wings from the cockpit fascinated me right away, the way you use the stick and foot pedals to move the elevator, the ailerons, and the rudder. They gave me a demonstration of how everything in the cockpit worked: the instruments that show if the engines are functioning properly, the instruments for flying and landing, the navigational aids, the tachometer and pressure gauges, the temperature and fuel gauges. Even back then, what I liked most were the airspeed indicator and the gyroscopic compass, which was in constant motion. And the feeling of floating above the earth! But I'm still afraid of flying, even today. The damage to our motor, by the way, was much more serious than my copilot and I thought at first. We didn't find out until a thorough inspection was done that our mix of oxygen and fuel was quite explosive. We were really lucky to be able to make an emergency landing so quickly."

He stretched out at full length, holding fast to the fatherhair. He looked up at the sky. In some places, the clouds were parted like curtains, revealing stars and the blinking of satellites circling the earth. The cloudless interstices looked like rivers. It was like looking out a plane window through rents in the clouds onto the landscape below—fields, rivers, villages.

After a long silence, he whispered, "Hold me Erin, please, hold me tight."

She laid a hand on his shoulder and just that much did him a world of good. She left her hand there. He turned his head toward it, kissed her slim fingers and the back of her hand.

"Lie down next to me, please, snuggle up to me. I've been longing for that since I first saw you."

"What next, I wonder," murmured Erin. Was she talking to herself or to him?

"Are you talking to me?" he asked.

Her hand still lay on his shoulder.

A wave washed over the metal surface, swamping the place where they lay. Erin jumped up with a little cry.

"You absolutely cannot stay here! Get up. Right now!"

He was rooted to the spot. "My father's fondest wish was to make it to the year 2000, and he was sure he would. He had no doubts. I'm going to live to be a hundred and twenty! he would proclaim, right up to the end. For as long as I can remember he would calculate for me how old he would be and how old I would be in the year 2000. He was convinced that starting in the year 2000, the world was going to be a better place. The year 2000 would mark the transition to a good era; it would be the gateway to a happier future. Maybe he was right. We'll know soon enough."

"Now listen to me, Gustav. We can't stay here. You're soaking wet. It looks like you've injured your foot. You aren't adequately dressed. If you don't get up this minute, you'll catch pneumonia."

"I have to say good-bye to him, Erin. Don't you understand? I have to say a last farewell. Once and for all. To be reborn, I have to bid Ludwig David Rubin farewell. That's why I'm lying here today. He's been waiting for me. The least I can do is spend the night with him, next to him. Just one last night. My everlasting childhood is ending tonight."

"I'm begging you to get up now. Please stand up. You've still got a long trip ahead of you."

But Gustav clung even more tightly than before to the gigantic skull of his father.

Whereupon, with a brisk, efficient gesture, Erin cast off and boarded the boat to go look for help in Tarrytown.

Not until the sound of her motor was dying away did Gustav suddenly stand up. He slipped, steadied himself on the fatherbrow, regained his balance. Then he called out across the river, "Please—come back! Come back to me!"

Erin couldn't understand what he'd called, but she came about.

Gustav turned one last time toward his father's face. Beloved Father, he whispered, forgive me. I'm going to save my life, the life you gave me.

He desecrated Shabbat, scrambled, stumbled, fell into the ferrywoman's boat. At that moment, it seemed to him more like a dugout canoe.

Peter Stephan Jungk was born in Los Angeles, raised in several European cities, and now lives in Paris. A former screenwriting fellow of the American Film Institute, he is the author in German of eight books, including the acclaimed biography *Franz Werfel: A Life from Prague to Hollywood* (Grove Press 1990) and the novels *Tigor* (Handsel Books, 2004), a finalist for the British Foreign Book Award, and *The Perfect American* (Handsel Books, 2004), a fictional biography of Walt Disney's last months, which Philip Glass is adapting into an opera that will open the New York City Opera's 2012–2013 season.

David Dollenmayer is Professor of German at Worcester Polytechnic Institute and the translator of works by Bertolt Brecht, Michael Kleeberg, Anna Mitgutsch, Perikles Monioudis, Mietek Pemper, and Moses Rosenkranz. He is the author of *The Berlin Novels of Alfred Döblin* and coauthor of *Neue Horizonte: A First Course in German Language and Culture*. He lives in Hopkinton, Massachusetts.